MURDER AT
BLACK
DRAGON
RIVER

By Bosley Wilder

Printed in Victoria, Canada

Note for Librarians: a cataloguing record for this book that includes Dewey Classification and US Library of Congress numbers is available from the National Library of Canada. The complete cataloguing record can be obtained from the National Library s online database at:
www.nlc-bnc.ca/amicus/index-e.html

ISBN 1-4120-1180-9

This book was published on-demand in cooperation with Trafford Publishing.

On-demand publishing is a unique process and service of making a book available for retail sale to the public taking advantage of on-demand manufacturing and Internet marketing. On-demand publishing includes promotions, retail sales, manufacturing, order fulfilment, accounting and collecting royalties on behalf of the author.

Suite 6E, 2333 Government St., Victoria, B.C. V8T 4P4, CANADA
Phone   250-383-6864   Toll-free 1-888-232-4444 (Canada & US)
Fax   250-383-6804   E-mail   sales@trafford.com
Web site www.trafford.com   TRAFFORD PUBLISHING IS A DIVISION OF TRAFFORD HOLDINGS LTD.
Trafford Catalogue #03-1558   www.trafford.com/robots/03-1558.html
10   9   8   7   6   5   4   3

For Alexa, Brittany and Emily
who also love to make up stories

Acknowledgments

I 've owed a debt of gratitude to many persons through the writing of this book.

For their expertise and advice, I am grateful to my editorial assistant Melissa Coogan, whose overall critiquing, judgment, loyalty, and familiarity with computer quirks is unbeatable; to friend Amy Hughes, whose editorial eye is surpassed only by her patience; to Bill and Jackie Van Voris, who sat encouragingly through long, firelit evenings of chapter readings, commenting wisely and always positively; to Geng Ping, who taught me how to spell current romanized Mandarin, and other Chinese virtues; Marjorie Kaufman, an early and thorough reader; Lyn Reale, who pointed out initial hurdles to be overcome;

Joni Walker, always knowledgeable and supportive; Michelle Bourne's invaluable help through makeup and layout; and to Pat and Gary Peterson, who listened to my musings, always delightfully serene with my blather.

Cover design by Charlotte Herring

All the characters, as well as the setting for this story, are entirely fictitious

"Reality is some amalgam of the see-er and the seen, or as the case may be, the unseen."

Stephen Dunn

Main Characters

Judith Treadway- an American foreign expert, teacher of American literature in the English Department of Shi Tong University in a city in northern China

Shelby Johnson- young, newly-arrived teacher in the English Department

Dr. Stanley Poussaint- semantics expert and Mandarin-speaking member of the foreign community at Shi Tong University

Zhang Jingchun- Chairman of the English Department, professes his love for Professor Treadway

Yang Youli- Director of the University's Foreign Affairs Unit

Wu Fang- newly arrived Chinese-American teacher, wife of Taylor Battle

Taylor Battle- young American teacher, married to Wu Fang

Xiao Mei- university student, secretly in love with Taylor Battle

Eileen Tryst- teacher, resents Professor Treadway's dominance in academic scene

Li Jien- top senior student at the University, willing to do anything to achieve his goal of going to the U.S.

Ling Feng- Chief Inspector, local police

Heavenly Fountain- University librarian

Chapter 1
Sunday Peace Disrupted

November.

Bicycling along the deserted pathway to Xin Lou Main Building of Shi Tong University in Shen Shang, China, Shelby Johnson, in her third month of teaching English on a foreign campus, far away from her Louisiana hometown, was luxuriating in the quiet and peacefulness of the morning. Black Dragon River, which ran along just below the bluffs at the edge of campus, glimmered in its sleek flow in the early morning sunlight. The sight of the quiet water heightened the young teacher's joy in what was being a serene weekend, free of appointments, academic or social.

She had initially complained to herself at having now to get dressed early and go out on a Sunday. If she hadn't forgotten on Friday afternoon to bring back the rest of her papers from the office she and Professor Judith Treadway shared, she wouldn't have to have gotten up and out, but could still be relaxing in her comfy bed.

She was not used to the emptiness and silence along the walkways of campus. She was much more accustomed to the weekday throngs of students dashing to or from classes along the pathway. Normally, riding among them, she often had the sense of playing one of those virtual Pokeman games, where a player had to anticipate the direction and speed of the walkers: estimating the distance between two groups, one of which she planned to pass. At times she would have to veer sharply to dodge those who, coming toward her, abruptly changed pattern or direction. Occasionally a student might leap out of step with a companion or a row of classmates walking together, just "fooling around," but causing her to brake sharply or cut to the right or left to avoid being "blown away" by the attacking monster. At the turn in the longish road, some students would make unannounced decisions to jump the curb and head along the diagonal path through the small courtyard, rather than continue straight to the main gate. All of these challenges kept one occupied while traversing the roadway between the Foreign Guest House, where she lived, and the University's Main Building, where she taught. To cycle the five hundred meters of road took about the same length of time required to play a video game, was just as much fun, and, while you didn't get to raise the flag, you also did not have to shell out fifty dollars for a new DVD, the way her sister did. She didn't play Pokeman games herself, of course, but considerable babysitting of her seven-year-old nephew back home in Louisiana had left Pokeman's resolute patterns indelibly printed in her head, even ten thousand miles away from home.

But today was Sunday. Everyone was still as a mouse, as grandmama would say. Last evening's campus noises of Saturday night drunken scholars on a spree—the students singing and brawling, the sound of breaking glass as another empty beer bottle, or one from *baijiu*, the local murderous white alcohol, was flung out of a window and hit the ground—had subsided, given way to the gentle chirp of a bird and the quiet of a Sunday morning. The University unit workers' empty buses were lined side by side in their corner parking lot, like sleeping cubs. In the distance, a solitary taxi swung around the corner and disappeared through the main gate into the silent street.

Arriving at Main Building, she climbed the stairs to her second-floor office and unlocked the door with the standard cheap aluminum key on her key ring. She fitted the key into the lock several times as she always had to; pushing to the left until the teeth found the correct notch that turned the bolt. She swore in exasperation at the time she wasted every day getting the damned door open. Xiao Hu, the Foreign Language Department Administrative Assistant, had promised to change the lock for her, but, in a bureaucracy the size of Mt. Everest, such a request was not a simple matter. It had to go through the University hierarchy, from Xiao Hu to his boss, the Chief of the Administrative Office, through the Dean of Administrative Affairs to the Department Chairman, through the Party Secretary to Central Administration, and thence through dear God knew whom else before reaching the Purchasing

Department. Probably, thought Shelby, it was on the agenda for several upcoming semi-weekly meetings. She could expect a new lock by next spring, if she lasted that long. Meanwhile, today it seemed harder than usual to hit the pins just right. She jabbed and pushed a few more times before feeling the tumblers give way. She pushed with her free arm to send the door swinging inward and wide open. Then she screamed.

She screamed again, at the top of her lungs, her book bag flying to the floor as she raised her hands to her face, cupping her eyes, and reeled backward through the door. What she was seeing was Judith Treadway sprawled in the chair at her desk near the window. The professor's head was flung back over the top of the chair, eyes wide open. Blood around the neck saturated her white silk blouse, the bow still neatly tied at her throat, which had been slashed. Judith's arms in their graceful silk dangled limp at the sides of the chair, which together with the spread-eagle legs gave the body the appearance of a ghoulish rag doll.

"Ai-ee! Ai-ee!" Shelby screamed.

"*Zenmele*? *Zenmele*? What happened?" The clerk Xiao Hu had run to the doorway of the office. "What's the matter, w-hat's going on, Jiu *Laoshi*?" He came forward into the room.

"Ai-eeee-!" The sounds coming from Shelby shrilled as she turned, horror freezing her face, and flung her arms around the startled Xiao Hu. Then, in an overwhelming need to vomit, she broke away and ran down the empty corridor to the women's toilet. She did not quite make it.

Hearing her screams, several *fuwuyuan*, the university charwomen, appeared in the hallway, one of them dragging her broom behind her as she ran toward the frenzied, retching woman. As in a nightmare, Shelby felt hands at her elbows, someone leading her down the corridor. Then she fainted.

Chapter 2
A Party for Newcomers

September.

Shelby Johnson and Elaine Tryst, newly appointed teachers at Shi Tong University in northern China, sat watching the student dancers like two junior high school teachers who had pulled duty as chaperones. Young Americans in their thirty's, the two women had some months ago each decided on her own to extend a teaching career with a year's contract in China. Now here they were in Shen Shang, in an awesomely strange part of the planet with a pleasant green university campus surrounded by a bustling, traffic-snarled market town. Elaine noted with some ingenuousness, given her reason for being hired to teach in China, that "nobody outside the University spoke English."

"Will you take a look at that!" At their table, at the side of the dance floor, Elaine nudged Shelby in the side as two of the Russian teacher experts, who appeared much more at home here than did the newly arrived Americans, did a sweating and bright, cheerful polka, in perfect double time to the metallic clatter coming out of the loudspeakers.

"Just what you came here to learn, isn't it, darlin'?" Shelby laughed.

Although the fall term had barely begun, the two women were well on the way to becoming good friends despite the huge differences in their personalities. Shelby was effervescent, open and easygoing, with her soft Louisiana accent. Elaine, who had been born biologically in Oregon but "born again" in her own religious terms, was frequently overtaken by the high seriousness of life. Her face had the dour expression of a disappointed latterday don. At this, the term's "getting together party", mostly for the many new students from Europe, Australia, and the U.S., the two women observed the newcomers with unfeigned interest. The entire mass of students present presumably would be doing academic work in the Chinese department, so was not really of academic interest to the English teachers. Nevertheless, everyone here in the hall tonight had been invited as part of the foreign languages departments of the University community.

The University's student dining room, converted for the night into a ballroom, glistened under the swirling light from the revolving kaleidoscope ball at the ceiling. These dozens of young foreign students who had come from their homes to far off Shen Shang, China, to attend Shi Tong University, gyrated with abandon in the motley splashes of prismatic reds, yellows, and greens of strobe light so spectral they seemed radioactive.

Exercising their rights to an early loss of hearing, the kids twisted and jerked to the loud pulsating beat coming from the rap CD—Snoop Dog, Shelby recognized—blaring over the loudspeakers.

Elbows askew, some moshed in the center of the dance floor, jingy; others hopped, with legs jerking; trucker rockers did a sort of polka to the rap beat. A good many of them wore fashionable shoes with those thick, clumpy soles and heels that looked like combat boots, but the heavy look belied the light, quick steps many of them manaaged. Comical how fashions change, Shelby was thinking. When she was in college, not so long age, actually, anyone wearing thick soles and heels like those was thought surely to have club feet or some other podiatric disability.

From Russia, Germany, the U.S. or Canada, the kids mixed and matched, getting acquainted in their own terms as they initiated themselves into pursuing a new kind of foreign language as well as an environment that involved certain new customs. The party in the ballroom of the Foreign Guest House, they were told, was to celebrate the new batch of foreign students as well as Autumn Festival. It was in full swing.

Yang Youli, the Director of the University's Foreign Affairs Unit, an office known by foreigners simply as the "Waiban," sat staid at another table to the side of the dance floor. He sipped at a bottled orange drink through a straw as he kept his eyes on the dancers. Not for nothing was Director Yang known privately as "Mr. Power." He wore well the invisible but recognizable crown of an administrator in China's established tradition of authoritarian government in the public sector. The man could also be counted upon to make the appropriate political gesture, in this case a party, lavish for China, aimed at inspiring reassurance in the foreign students that their arrival in his great country under the University's special student exchange program was a unique life opportunity, heralded tonight by the festive occasion sponsored for their pleasure by his University's Foreign Affairs Unit. As befitted a modern emperor, he was flanked by a deputy and a gofer, as well as by several of the University's official interpreters. The job of the latter was to facilitate the civil if stiff pleasantries carried on between the various guests and their host, Yang Youli, whose sole language was Mandarin Chinese, despite his politically important position as Foreign Affairs Director. In less surreal light, this stern-looking table of chaperones might have had a dampening effect upon the merrymaking. As it was, there existed a notable empty space on the dance floor in the area adjacent to the executive table.

In another area of the crowded ballroom, Dr. Judith Treadway, American and senior foreign expert in the English Department, and Professor Stanley Poussaint, linguistics specialist from Canada, did a relaxed two-step along the sidelines, Poussaint doing his best to steer his dance partner clear of the more irrepressible elements in the bobbing crowd.

"I hope you're impressed!" he shouted to Judith over Christina Aguilera's pulsing song, "with my skill in keeping you from being trampled!" Just in time, he guided her out of the path of a twosome who appeared to incorporate elements of the tango in their otherwise state-of-the-art discotheque performance.

Although the Foreign Guest House was for social purposes generally off-limits to Chinese national students, a few during this busy evening had talked their way in or crept unnoticed past the *fu tai*, the receptionists and guardians of the gate. Most of those who had gotten in past security kept themselves as far out of sight of Director Yang Youli and the Waiban as possible. At a table in the far corner of the room, they sat eyeing the foreigners, and giggling among themselves, female students decorously holding their hands in front of their mouths.

But not all of today's young Chinese were socially as docile as the students of a dozen years ago, Stanley observed to himself with some amusement as he looked out over the room. A few native youngsters moved openly onto the floor, inhibitions flung to the winds as they imitated the free street dancing and jamming of the Westerners and Overseas Chinese students from Hong Kong and Singapore, or other countries outside the Motherland. At one table, a half dozen students ignored the beat of a Britney Spears lyric now coming from the loudspeakers, as they clapped and sang in rhythm their own folksong in Chinese. Marching to their own drum, Stanley Poussaint thought, taking wry pleasure in this ingenious expression of individuality.

A few of the female foreign students had put on dresses for the party. But the majority of the dancers, male and female, wore jeans and colored T-shirts with the usual emblems from Red Sox to home university icons to more iconoclastic statements like "Metalhead." In the great student revolts for individualism and freedom of choice, that choice, as far as fashion was concerned, appeared to be a uniform of jeans, some ragged, and T-shirts, or sweatshirts, that overall displayed the vast assortment of stenciled advertisements, jokes or geographical designations so popular in the world's consumer cultures. Few persons under age twenty-five had the temerity to be seen without some items of the requisite Levi-type blue denim textile as part of their clothing, be it pants or jacket. Stanley had to smile as he reflected how these items of clothing largely had made the journey from a clothing factory in China to a far part of the world to journey back with their student owners to the country of origin.

A young Asian woman wearing a single long black pigtail down her back had circled the ballroom at least four times during the current Mariah Carey vocal, dancing a solo variety of dance figures as she kicked high like a cancan dancer, swiveled her upper torso and her head like a South Indian Kathakali, then whirled like a Mongolian folk dancer. Completely absorbed in herself, she appeared from the movements of her mouth to be singing, although it was of course impossible to hear anything over the electronic blast. Her short, box-like figure was in curious contradiction to her elongated dance figures.

She extended her arms and legs as though she were trying to get out of a body whose shape did not quite accommodate her need for unique expression.

Back at their table, Elaine shifted her gaze to the doorway. "Here comes Dr. Zhang," she said to Shelby. "Do you suppose he's going to ask us to dance?" she mouthed with the smallest undertone of mirth.

"Why, I'll ask him!" Shelby exclaimed in a high voice, then did her best to appear solemn as Zhang Jingchun, the chairman of the Foreign Language Department, headed toward them. Dr. Zhang's own specialty was English, one of the half dozen foreign languages offered by the University, which also specialized in Russian, Japanese, and to a lesser extent, French and German.

"Are you finding the evening interesting?" Dr. Zhang motioned to a chair next to Elaine, and, at a polite nod from her, sat down at the table with the two women.

"I don't know if you'd care to dance with me, Dr. Zhang." Shelby's eyes twinkled with mischief. It was well known that Dr. Zhang did not dance.

"You young ladies are young enough to trip the light fantastic without me," he replied in his clear, studied English as he gestured toward the dancers.

A kind man, Dr. Zhang chaired the department with the discipline the system demanded as well as with the private sensitivities of a fine human being. He carried within him the emotional scars of the Great Cultural Revolution of the mid-twentieth century. It was common knowledge around the University how as a very young man, he had been twice imprisoned, for no greater offense than the ability to write lyric poetry. During those horrific years, his young wife had died in the freezing outer farmland where teachers and other intellectuals had been sent for "re-education," the penalty imposed on those who occasionally did their own thinking. That re-education appeared to consist largely of cleaning latrines on the rural communes.

Dr. Judith Treadway and Professor Stanley Poussaint glided over to where the two young instructors were sitting. As they approached the table, Dr. Zhang stood up to greet them.

"Please, please," said Judith Treadway, motioning for him to sit back down. Noticing that the local TV crew had arrived, she pointed over to them and sighed. In a few minutes, she knew, one of the officials from the Waiban would come over and ask her to dance. A slow waltz or foxtrot would enable the cameramen to record the diplomacy of a local government official courteously "dancing with a foreign expert," a standard for this kind of TV news feature. Stanley Poussaint would probably be asked for a comment on the arrival of the great number of new foreign students from many nations, the kind of media request that usually drove him to threaten to hide in a telephone booth. It was difficult for him to remain genial, he remarked to Judith, with "those camcorders in my face," but he'd try to keep being a good diplomat.

"Hello, everyone," Stanley greeted Shelby and Elaine, and reached to shake hands with Dr. Zhang. They all sat at the table to watch the dancers under the kaleidoscopic lighting, bright banners and the rows of international flags that hung overhead. "How's it going?"

"My God! Look at that!" Elaine nudged Shelby with her elbow, at the printing on an Asian-looking student's T-shirt, *Bust me, Baby*. "You'd think they'd know better than to wear something like that in China."

Shelby smiled. "Ah don't think a Chinese would have one clue what it meant."

"Well, it's indecent."

The blaring Nelly CD came to an end. After a few minutes, a surprising new, temperate lyric sound emerged as the voice of Frank Sinatra took over the speakers in "I Left my Heart in San Francisco."

"Why, that's a real oldie!" Judith exclaimed. "Stanley, don't you know this?" She nodded in the direction of a nearby loudspeaker.

"Sure," Stanley grinned. "My mother loved it. Care to try again, Judith? If my knees don't creak too loud."

Across the ballroom floor, Wang Xiao Mei, in her second year as a student at Shi Tong University, accompanied by a graduate student from the Economics Department, diffidently but determinedly initiated the steps of the dancers in her vicinity, throwing her arms into the air as she shuffled, as though she knew exactly what she was doing. She noticed the English Department Chairman Zhang talking with the foreign teachers. She quickly nudged her partner so that her own face was turned away from that direction. She was not supposed to be here, she knew. But the *futai* on duty was a friend of the graduate student, who himself was her own father's cousin's son, so of course he had let them through the door.

Xiao Mei had learned a great deal about the workings of the world since she had been selected from all the students in her own village secondary school to enter the examinations for university admission. She alone had been selected to attend Shi Tong University for training as a future English teacher. Now she was here, dancing in this huge dance room. She, Xiao Mei, no longer a girl, but a mature woman, who had come to know life and love hardly dreamed of before these past few wonderful weeks at university. She looked up at the strobe light, feeling as though she was doing arabesques on an imaginative level.

Xiao Mei was very happy. In this room, she could share yet another small part of life with her yellow-haired loved one, whom she could see through the crowd across the room as he politely danced with another of the foreign students. HE and SHE did not dare to acknowledge each other publicly; they had to keep their love secret. But perhaps it would not be for long. Her tall, handsome beloved had given her his sweet smile once earlier this evening. The smile, held and memorized in the flashes of the white strobe light, would feed her thoughts and envelop him, until she could be with him again.

She brought her hand up to touch her face, as her lover had the other night while a fingernail of a moon had shown above them. It had been so warm when they lay in the grass together. Enfolded in her lover's arms, she had felt as though she were home in her own dreams in her own countryside. Hypnotized by the moonlight, she had found joy in his strength and wonderful love. That tiny bit of moon had been a symbol in the darkness of their love, which would grow and grow, she knew. She lay in his arms, his masculinity overcoming her, so painful, so sweet!

What would her beloved grandmother, who had brought her up in strict tradition in their village, say when she found out how her granddaughter had felt such joy as her lover Taylor had come to know her. Ever since she had begun to stay alone after class when she knew she loved her blue-eyed teacher and he loved her. Their love had grown with each passing day. The other evening, as they had arranged again to meet secretly outside, he had caressed her hair, and touched her, touched parts of her body that no one, not even herself, knew.

"*Wo ai ni!*" She breathed into his ear.

"I love you, too, Xiao Mei. I love you."

That he was a foreigner was not important. He was HE, and she was SHE. Nothing could stand in the way of their love, nothing else mattered. She surprised herself by recognizing that she would kill, if necessary, to maintain this beautiful, lucky love that had been given them. She wanted to tell grandmother about it. Of all people in the world, she felt that Grandma would understand.

She, Xiao Mei, had worked so hard to get into University, to have a future. She smiled. Who would have known this great love was to be her future? Her smile had erupted into a whispered, happy murmur.

"What did you say, my darling?"

"*Wo ai ni - -* my darling." The English "my darling" felt strange on her tongue. But she would get used to calling him that. Xiao Mei smiled to herself as she reflected she was learning many new phrases of the English language that were not in her textbooks.

"You are my perfect one, my gentle princess. You are the most perfect princess in the world. All mine." He tightened his arms about her.

"You are my prince. My master."

They had lain for a long time together in the grass, hands entwined. The earth beneath them was sweet, the fingernail moon above obscured for a moment by a passing cloud. The lights from the windows of an undergraduate dormitory at the end of the campus road several yards away from where they lay were almost all extinguished. It was close to eleven o'clock curfew time at his dorm.

After some minutes, they had stood, shaking the leaves from their clothes. Holding each other tenderly, they had kissed once more, then parted, each heading in the direction of their separate housing.

Tonight, after another look over the crowded dance floor to spot her beautiful lover just one more time, she turned to her cousin and politely requested that they leave. It was getting late. Her dormitory would be closing soon. It was important that she observe the curfew rules, and not get into trouble.

Chapter 3
Ponderings

On this Saturday afternoon in late October, the sky was just beginning to grow dark. Around the quadrangle of Shi Tong University, the first lamps being turned on in rooms in the student dormitories had begun to illuminate the dim, redbrick rectangles like giant lightboards. Professor Judith Treadway, dressed in a burgundy pantsuit of light wool and wearing white Nike running shoes, shifted the brown leather briefcase from her right to her left hand to ease the weight on her right shoulder, and walked with her customary determined step across campus, heading over the common toward the Foreign Experts Guest House. As she walked, she felt the batch of senior term papers in the briefcase weigh her down. It must be all the heavy thinking that went into those papers. She smiled to herself. Certainly judging from the number she had read in her office since lunch time on this quiet weekend afternoon, a good deal of effort had gone into these academic exercises.

Being the last major papers the seniors wrote before midterm ended, they certainly were important. By November, the Department would be calling for tentative, estimated grade figures, so that planning could begin on which seniors would be selected for graduate work following this year's graduation of the young teachers' class. The selections were heavily weighted in favor of the students most skilled in written, formal language, often without regard to their personalities or abilities to handle the rigors of teaching. Selection for academia was nevertheless an intellectual plum for the student as well as a great social prize to the parents of a potential *Laoshi*, respected teacher.

Quite a number of the students in this graduating class had expressed interest in graduate study, Judith Treadway reflected. It was part of her job to analyze the why's and the wherefore's of that interest. Some young people on graduating from college just wanted to get into the job market, particularly these days when increasingly they had more freedom in their socialist system to choose careers in a society more open to private economic development than in previous years. Some seemed genuinely bent on pursuing additional literary or linguistic research for two or three years more. During that time they prepared themselves for a teaching career and, if matriculated here at the University, were even permitted to teach a few beginning classes of incoming freshman.

Of course, in every striving scholar lay the fond hope of eventually going abroad for study. What dreams! And a frequent phrase in the vocabulary of every Chinese student was the "going abroad for study," brief or long, and preferably long, in the West. "The West" meant most often the United States (referred to as simply "America"), or Canada, Australia or England. Many students went for a year, or two. Some, in the past had been lucky enough to stay on for their Ph.D's. Additionally, in today's new economic atmosphere, it was possible to return, help their own country improve economically while making money in a business career themselves. Some had found jobs which allowed them to work in both countries. There were also those who went for freedom, a new life, never to return, although that desire of course never appeared in their written applications for a visa. So many dreams, many unspoken, not uncommon.

It was also one of Professor Treadway's functions as a foreign expert to be instrumental in the selection of a number of students who would be fortunate enough to continue their studies abroad in the coming year. Shi Tong University, known for short as Shi Da ("School of Higher Education"), had been the sister university of Michigan's Mohegan University for the past twenty years. Judith looked upon the Chinese institution with particular fondness. It was her home away from home. She had begun to teach there as a young Ph. D. She mused that her retirement, technically, when it came, would be from Mohegan, but a large part of her heart as well as her career, was here at Shi Da. Part of her duties comprised teaching at this sister university in China and administering the U.S. end of the scholarship exchange program. Although candidates were officially initiated by the Chinese head of the local

English department and subject to approval by Beijing, it was understood on campus that is was Professor Treadway who made the real choices.

She herself had done all she could to discourage that notion. In fact, she had on several occasions requested that her own university give more power to the Chinese in the final say of which two candidates a year got to go abroad. But, the governing body of her institution, having been burned on a few occasions in the past decade by the arrival on the Mohegan campus of politicians' sons or daughters whose English was limited to "How do you do?" and whose academic ability consisted almost exclusively in the knowledge of how to move a ping pong ball from one side of a table to the other, was in no way partial to any further diplomatic or political liquidation of its funds. Judith was stuck with the unpleasant task of designating winners from the senior class. She took it in stride, however, scrutinizing with complete candor and academic honesty the skills and potential defined by her own school's guidelines. She made her decisions and recommendations with complete integrity, often after much agonizing.

She was agonizing right now, as she walked across the campus. It was not at all a pleasurable task, making these selections. Considered a fine, if strict, teacher, she was fond of all her students. With a few exceptions over the years, she had wished great success for each of them. Sometimes, she felt, with a guilty twinge, that she was even more concerned about her students in China than she was about those back in America. The choices for success and certain kinds of happiness were so much more limited here than they were at home. Her students here very often had little or no choice in the selection of a future career, or even a current job. Their native towns and villages and local politics and economies often dictated a student's job search. Although economic choice was much more open since the late Deng Xiaoping's direction of China's economic policies, there were still political holdovers in effect from the past. It was discouraging that most young people had been thrust earlier into study categories of science or mathematics or the liberal arts simply as the results of tests given them in elementary school, and certainly without consideration of their own wishes or even knowledge of choices for lifetime careers.

A youngster eight or nine years old who happened to score high on a math or science test unconsciously decreased his chances of ever being allowed to become a writer or musician. He was earmarked for the sciences or an engineering career. Conversely, a student with rich verbal skills would find it frustrating to dream of becoming an architect. Before her tenth birthday, the official state selection process likely had her frozen into Interpreter Position #1705682. Such was the system since the inception of socialist China, or "Socialism with a Chinese flavor," as it was termed.

But such facts made it even more important that she choose as candidates for advanced study abroad those whose talents would be of intellectual and social benefit to themselves, their university, and to the future as a whole, insofar as a guideline as tenuous as "the future" could be defined as more than dreamy idealism. But at least she could try to choose between those candidates who wanted to return to help their country become even more of a world success and those who challenged themselves primarily for their own personal gain.

A sudden chill wind nipped through her thin wool jacket. It would be November shortly. Winter was coming. Winters in northeastern China were no picnic. Temperatures fell to twenty-five degrees below zero, occasionally even lower, to minus forty degrees Fahrenheit. And the currents from the Gobi Desert brought the wind chill factor to a point that occasionally made being outdoors a most uncomfortable, if not painful, experience.

She, like the other foreigners, was grateful that the Foreign Guest House was unusually warm and comfortable at this time of year. The local Foreign Affairs Office on campus did make the effort to accommodate its foreign teachers. The radiators in the Foreign Guest House had already been turned on in mid-October, a full two weeks ahead of the local faculty and student dormitories, which remained in their natural condition of temperature chills.

Brrrh, how she wished they'd start heating the classrooms, too. Judith shivered at the thought of the cold in that building. Her students had begun to bundle up in heavy sweaters and coats. Soon everyone would be wearing long underwear and the several layers of clothing that added extra pounds, and gave the campus the appearance of being peopled drolly by animated snowmen. She should have worn a heavier sweater under her jacket today; but the sun shining in through the windows of her office had been warm. The sun had set now, leaving only a light orange-rose scrawl beyond the heavy elm trees.

"Good evening, Treadway *Laoshi*!"

"Good evening!" Judith smiled as she acknowledged the greeting in the appropriate Mandarin for "respected teacher" of a few students who passed her on their way to the canteen. They carried with them their tin food pails to collect their dinners, which they would cart back to their dorms for consumption. Ah, to be young and not care about cold food or cold weather, she thought. But she corrected her reaction. It wasn't a question of caring about alternatives. These students had not been exposed to other conditions of comfort, so, at least theoretically, they were well adjusted to their environment.

Classes had been in session for almost six weeks now. Judith was able to recognize by sight most of the students in her two classes of American literature. With eighteen to twenty students in a class, it was not too difficult to recall faces. To memorize forty Chinese names, most of which had three syllables, the initial one being the family name, was a more difficult matter for a foreigner.

Even though she taught classes in what was to the students a foreign literature, and in a foreign language, she liked to use the students' Chinese names, not just Helen or Willy, or Patsy - or Lord, forbid, some outrageous name that a teacher in a lower grade, or the student, had inflicted on himself. Some had names like Napoleon, or Pillsbury (where do they get them?) or, in one case, Undercover. In the latter case, she had felt compelled to advise the young man that "Undercover" was not a common name in the western hemisphere, much less one that could be used in most social situations without remark or curiosity, let alone some hilarity. She had strongly suggested a name change to the young lady who had chosen as her English name "Crinkle," because her favorite foreign teacher two years ago had told her that her "face got all crinkled" when she smiled. The girl had felt that observation a lovely compliment.

Among the group of students who had greeted her and who walked ahead of her now, she recognized Wang Jing and Wang Rui, two very bright and conscientious young women who always arrived to class early and who sat at the two desks immediately in front of her own teacher's podium. They took copious notes during Professor Treadway's lectures (and presumably during their other professors', too), writing in tandem and continuously checking the other's notes. They explained that they always studied together, so each one took half their class notes. "Two heads are better than one!" they exclaimed during a conference, at which they had appeared together as they explained their study habits to her.

Walking alone behind them, a plastic lunch box neatly under one arm and carrying a large hot water thermos, the symbiotic twins, as she thought of them, was that minority student in her first section, Bhong Taur. From. . . Mongolia?. . . one of the outlying northern regions. A serious, studious young man, he, too, sat at the front of the room, and seemed to hang on her every word. She had talked with him only once. Bhong Taur was shy, as ninety percent of her students were, but astonishingly articulate once he began asking questions about class work, or just discussing aspects of literature. She must find out more about him.

Someone behind her hawked and spat, making a sound still not uncommon in China, despite huge legal efforts to curb the habit, especially in the cities. Even after the number of trips she had made here in the past decade- - five now, wasn't it? - - she still winced every time she heard the offensive throat-clearing, *haw-aw-k*, fearing that the end result of it might just land on her. China was a great and wonderful country, and she loved it. Only the uninhibited spitting, and of course the occasional stench of some not-cleaned-frequently-enough *cesuo*, toilets, practically disturbed her enjoyment of this rich, ancient civilization high wiring the rim of the twenty first century. Fortunately, health and sanitation measures had been improving each year since Deng Xiaoping's economic development plan had first been instituted.

"Judith, you aren't going to dinner tonight? It's five after five. We won't have time for any aperitif this evening." Dr. Poussaint was hurrying up the walk from behind her. She smiled. He always looked worried when he thought he was going to miss his dinner. Not infrequently, he would stop by her flat, or she, his, late in the afternoon for a glass of wine or a cup of tea, to relax and talk over the day's classes or particular questions or problems, or just listen to some music. Earlier, they had gone down to the canteen to dinner together at these times. Now, at five, if they happened to be together in her apartment, he could be counted on to rise punctually from his chair, saying, "Excuse me, it's dinner time. You know how *they* are," (he would say, with a wink of amusement) and leave her to the music while she finished whatever they had managed as hors d'oeuvres, or stay in her apartment to cook her own dinner. Not that he cared for the food. He just couldn't be bothered to cook anything for himself, although the new foreign faculty apartments boasted more than adequate small kitchens.

Now catching up with her on the path he said, "Oh, I forgot, you've stopped eating dinner in the canteen. You prefer to concoct your own gourmet treats. What is it tonight, turtle soup?" The ease between them invited comradely teasing, no offense meant or taken.

"My professional attentiveness doesn't extend through a canteen dinner hour unless I'm dragged there," Judith replied laughing. "You know that."

Stanley Poussaint shrugged. "It beats trying to fry your own eggs." He was panting slightly as he strode along. It did not keep him from making a sour face.

"What happened to your bicycle? How come you're walking?" She quickened her step to try to keep up with him now, in his hurry to get to the canteen, but he was getting ahead of her, still talking.

"I had to go downtown to a meeting this afternoon, so I left the bike at the Arts building. Anyway, it's good to walk. Good for the health. Listen, I have to hurry. See you later." He clipped on up the road in a part-jog, part dogtrot looking as though he were trying to imitate a mechanical wind-up toy. The rays of late afternoon sun caught his pate and the thinning red-gold hair surrounding it like a halo.

He nearly tripped over the broken neck of a glass bottle half-protruding from the dirt path, and was heard to emit a loud "Damn!. . ." It *was* irritating-- the students' carelessness about litter. Paper wrappers from snacks, broken bottles, and the empty containers from yogurt or milk drinks lay scattered on the ground. The government had some time ago passed several health and trash removal laws, but these had not yet filtered down completely to overrule popular custom. Rubbish often lay where it fell for days, including empty beer and soda bottles tossed jauntily to the ground from dormitory windows, usually with enough playful force to shatter the glass. Nor were the interiors of buildings sacrosanct. She recalled one day walking down a corridor of Xin Lou, the Main Building, to come upon two students stomping in turn on an empty bottle, apparently competing to smash it. As they stomped, they shouted, "*Haowanrr!*" . . . "Great fun!" It was dangerous fun. . .

Nevertheless, she admitted to herself, she loved China. She had the feeling of real accomplishment in her efforts here.

Stanley Poussaint, walking briskly ahead of Judith Treadway to try to get to canteen dinner on time so that he would not have to fry eggs for himself, was also thinking of his students. They were such an eager bunch, and for the most part, committed overachievers.

He nodded at some underclassmen who passed him now on the way to their own dinners, the young men for the most part sweet-faced and ingenuous, the young women pretty and with that appearance of slim fragility many Asian women possess, a quality made more arresting by the current fashion in short skirts and high-heeled shoes, which many of the young ladies wore even on the athletic field! It must take some doing to toss a shotput twenty-five feet while wearing three-inch heels, Stanley reflected with a grin. Nevertheless, a few girl students had mastered the challenge.

Curiously, in matters of student dress, the authorities were absolutely lenient: as long as modesty maintained itself, all kinds of previously labeled "decadent capitalist" fashions now prevailed on campus. Blue jeans were a favorite, worn with T-shirts and the fashionable longer cabin jacket by those who could afford one. As long as the weather held out, many of the young women preferred the feminine look of the very short skirt and high-heeled shoes. A few sported ankle socks with the high-heeled footwear, giving the wearer a unique Chinese fashion look. At least one out of the three young ladies sported stylishly bobbed hair and pretty earrings rather than the traditional pigtails or long straight hair hanging down the back of not too many years ago.

The students were hard-working and keen to succeed. Within their still-limited horizons, or perhaps because of them, they pursued new knowledge in ways their American counterparts, with their far greater opportunities, often did not bother. Student assignments here were completed on time without requests for extensions. Classes were attended with punctuality. There were, of course, the classical cases of excuses for repeated absence resulting from family members' presumed illnesses or deaths, used more often than not by weak or failing members of a class. A few years ago, one young man's father's elder brother died three times in one semester, requiring the nephew to return home for the funeral. In the springtime, the general need for a student to be excused from class especially for family or personal emergencies, increased in proportion to the pleasantness of the weather.

But in his seven consecutive years as a foreign expert in linguistics in the English Department at Shi Tong, a record that had earned him the honorific of Dean of the foreign community, Stanley Poussaint had encountered few chronic idlers. Laziness was not a Chinese characteristic. Most Chinese were practical, proper, and punctilious. Which reminded him, he had better hustle along even faster if he wanted to find anything still hot and decent to eat in the canteen. It was usually "careers open to talent," as Napoleon would say. He broke into a jog, briefcase bumping his chest.

Judith continued her slow walk, enjoying the evening. She would fix herself a sandwich in her small, but adequate, kitchen. She needed to concentrate on reading carefully and marking the remainder of the senior students' term papers. One or two of those she had read this afternoon she had put aside without grading. Occasionally, a student had to have a wrist slapped for copying out parts of a passage of a source book but forgetting an attribution. Innocent plagiarism? Sometimes. Occasionally deliberate cheating occurred. One paper in particular in the batch in her briefcase had left her with a distinct impression of her having read it in its entirety somewhere before. Perhaps she had just grown tired of reading the same subject matter over and over in the students' handwriting. She would have to re-read all those papers about which there might be a problem of any kind: questionable research, poor writing, and inadequate or inaccurate bibliography. Some students were just careless, as were some of her students back at Mohegan. Others pleaded innocence of the rules, which might not be a crime, but certainly prevented them from earning any but a very mediocre grade in the course. Then, of course, there were those who cheated, who hoped to get along with great gain for little pain. What a nuisance that lot was! She hoped she could get through this batch of theses without more than the usual friction and stress.

During the increasing twilight of the evening, lights had come on in all dormitories. As Judith continued along the darkening pathway, she felt lucky, not dissatisfied with her life. During her several tenures here at Shi Tong in the past ten years, she knew she had been able both to lay the foundation for a friendly, diplomatic academic relationship between her U.S. university and the Chinese "sister" university, and to establish a strong personal rapport with the necessary local functionaries, the members of the Foreign Language Department with whom she worked, and, of course, her numerous students. She felt she was respected but considered friendly by most students, even though she intimidated some of the more diffident or lazy. The latter mode, after all, provided its own incentive for those who needed to work more diligently. A certain manner of formal respect accorded her by some students occasionally embarrassed her - she found it difficult to accept elaborate kudos and compliments paid her by students and colleagues that she knew were mere polite form. The Chinese were probably the most polite people on the planet, which occasionally made it difficult to probe beneath the surface to learn what they really thought and felt. Not only was a guest always right, the surface was always smooth, the face impassive, until violence erupted. Not for nothing had the adjective "inscrutable" been applied generically by Westerners to the Chinese culture until it had become a cliché. There was always, in the words of the poet, "something unspoken between us." Face saving, for a Chinese as necessary as daily rice, provided a mask behind which enormous emotions and intentions remained well hidden.

Well, enough philosophizing, Judith told herself as she kicked a leaf. Practical everyday problems had to find solutions. She continued her walk through the fallen golden leaves of autumn until she reached the Foreign Guest House, where she climbed the two flights of stairs to her flat, the elevator being, as usual, dead.

Chapter 4
Wang Xiao Mei Is Unhappy

Wang Xiao Mei was crying. She sat on one of the side benches under the trees on the quadrangle. It was cold. She had come hurriedly out of her dormitory, almost at a run, fearing that her sobs would become loud before she could get out of earshot of her roommates. She had to get away, to be alone to think; she could not stand another minute of being confined in that small room with seven other girls. The four double bunks in the room were lined up two to each wall. Trunks, suitcases, and dressers filled all of the free space in the long, narrow, crowded room, with only a small aisle down the center. She felt fortunate to have a lower bunk near the door.

Oh! She suddenly had a thought that brought on a renewed burst of sobs. What if she had had an upper bunk, out of which she had to scramble so quickly and run down the hall to the common lavatory these past few mornings when she had those sick feelings in her gut? Would she have made it? As it was, she could barely get out the door and down the hall before the need to vomit got out of control, and she stood relieving herself in the cold, drafty open toilet room.

She had told her roommates she had *ganmao*, a bad cold, and an upset stomach. But today had been the fourth morning! She had not bled for many weeks now. Her grandmother had told her about these events in a woman's life. How much longer could she have this sickness happening to her every morning before her roommate insisted she go to the clinic for her "bad cold" or, worse? Fresh tears fell freely onto her navy blue coat. What if the others began to suspect the real cause of her misery! Perhaps they already suspected and were talking about her behind her back. What's more, she sobbed to herself, she had no privacy, and could not keep this terrible secret much longer. Some urgent action must be taken. She was confident her prince would rescue her as soon as he realized how serious the situation was. She looked at her watch. She had a class in ten minutes. She would write to him during class, so he would have her letter by noon.

Having made her decision, she felt better. She stood up and went hurriedly across the quadrangle to her dormitory to fetch her books and papers and get on to her classroom building.

Chapter 5
Taylor and Woofy Make Love

Woofy, Taylor's pet name for Wu Fang, sat crossed-legged in the sun on the floor of their bedroom in the Foreign Guest House. Her Conversational Mandarin textbook was propped against a stack of books in front of her. On her lap was a notebook into which she was carefully transcribing Chinese characters. The ideography of Mandarin was far from unfamiliar to her. She remembered Saturday morning Chinese language classes in Philadelphia as part of her traditional Chinese childhood, maintained even though her family had moved to America when she was seven years old. In high school, she had made every effort to undo all she had learned in her childhood of Chinese culture, in favor of becoming a french-fries-eating, gum-snapping, rebellious American teenager. Not too long ago, however, she had begun to regret having other than perfection in the Chinese language she had once rejected out-of-hand. Today, more mature, she considered it part of her duty as a Chinese-American woman of the twenty-first century, to master the language of her origins.

Looking over at Taylor, her sweet but lackadaisical husband stretched out on their bed, she watched him thumbing through some CD's, his boom box on the night table beside him. She bridled. Why did she always have to push him to work? He was so laid back, nothing seemed to excite him or inspire him. He was content to lie around half the day looking through magazines or playing his CD's. He did what he had to do, teaching his English grammar courses at the University, tutoring a few students. But he seemed to have no ambition to further himself in life. Why bother? His attitude seemed to be, Life is sweet, and I have everything I need, why strain beyond daily existence?

To Wu Fang, it was she who organized their lives. But the voice with which she addressed him betrayed none of her anger. Chinese-American women were cool.

"Taylor, honey—" Her voice was pitched high, but smooth and slow, as though she were reading a paragraph in a language she enjoyed but did not quite understand. He was really a beautiful man, with his blond hair and his soft grey eyes, round and sweet as a panda's. She wondered if a child of theirs would have his round eyes or her elliptical ones. Oh, if only she could get pregnant!

At the sound of her voice, Taylor looked up abstractedly from contemplation of the discs. As he turned his face toward his wife, he beamed the smile of a major toothpaste advertisement.

"Taylor," now her voice was teasing, but in a way he found exceedingly sexy. "Woofy is going to come and spank your bottom if you don't put those things away and get to work on your Mandarin—"

Taylor luxuriated at the sound of her voice. "Oh, she is, is she?"

He was on her in a second, the discs flung onto the floor as he sprang out of his chair and splayed himself over her, knocking the notebook out of her hand and pushing her shoulders to the floor. He buried his face in her hair, which she had swiftly loosened from its pins. He was feeling under her sweater for her breasts with one hand, with the other tugging at the snap of her jeans until the metal fastener popped, freeing her waist.

She pulled her jeans down around her knees, and was softly moaning now, rubbing her hair against his face. She moved her head down to his shoulder, and bit him, hard. In a moment, they were rolling over, one on top of the other; then she was down on him, burrowing like a puppy dog, lowering his jeans with her head and teeth. She could be fantastic when she wanted to be! Her hair was all over him, tickling. He ran his fingers through it, a liquid stream. . . .

While Taylor lay spread-eagled and snoring, Wu Fang curled at his side, her right arm supporting her head as she watched her husband. In a short while, she knew he'd awaken and she could entice him into their bi-weekly Chinese language lesson. On reflection, she knew herself the superior member of the pair. Observing him now with a kind of maternal tenderness, she told herself she was right to upbraid him for his mental laziness and lack of discipline. If it were not for her, he would still be sitting back in

Philadelphia, playing Play Station Two on his computer rather than learning to be an English teacher, working on his novel, and learning Mandarin. Having this great adventure in China! It was she who had inspired him to begin to learn Chinese, to want to come to China. He felt his Woofy was an incredible person. Inside herself she knew his assessment of her was who she really was, but most of the time she tried to keep herself a docile-appearing sweet wife. At least on the surface she kept her temper, her ambitions, even her many resentments against life, under control, a secret she shared with no one.

Smiling to herself, she slid gently from the bed and put on her slippers. She tiptoed into the living room, where she extracted a cigarette from a package high on a shelf, and some matches. She went out onto their small balcony. Taylor didn't like smoking in the apartment. He really didn't like her smoking at all.

They had met at a Writer's Workshop at Temple University, where Taylor was taking a course in creative writing. At first he had thought her aggressive; but he quickly began to feel that what seemed like toughness to others was really her bravery. She was not afraid to face opposition. She certainly had plenty of that! Her parents, immigrants from Taiwan twenty-five years ago, had tried to bring her up in a manner their generation considered proper for a female child of good family. Her mother had passed down all the domestic skills: cooking, sewing, the nurturing of younger children. She herself had almost single-handedly, taken care of her two younger brothers and a sister, as a traditional "elder sister" was expected to do. But her parents' ambitions for Wu Fang to marry a "nice Chinese boy" of her own class, preferably a doctor or a rich businessman, had met with rejection in their daughter's absolute absorption and immersion in becoming an American teenager. As soon as she was big enough not to fear being beaten by her father, she had promptly chopped her hair short, gone into mini-skirts, and exercised all the teenage hostility she was capable of, including running away one summer to "experience life."

As luck would have it, when she returned home to Philadelphia six months later, after a fulfilled, if miserable, experience in the adolescent runaway scene in New York, it was to find that, during her absence, her father had been taken ill and died. From that time onward she had the heavy responsibility of taking care of her mother. But Wu Fang still managed to go to college, on scholarships and financial aid she cadged from every available quarter. Her hair again grown long in the "let-it all-hang-out" fashion, she found time to become a political activist for women's rights.

She recalled how proud Taylor had been to march around City Hall with her, carrying posters advocating equal job opportunities. At home he was treated as lord and master, except for the occasional scolding she felt obliged to administer privately. As for their public life, he repeatedly told her how proud he was that she considered herself a point person for diversity for Chinese and other disenfranchised minority women. She was quick to assert the struggle for equality in this white, male, crony-ridden world.

Finishing her cigarette, she carefully stubbed the butt into the small tin can she kept on the porch behind her plants. She went back inside. The door squeaked as she closed it. She heard Taylor calling from their bedroom,

"Woofy? What time is it, Woofy?" She found him reaching sleepily for the clock.

"It's alright, baby. It's still early."

Let him sleep another ten minutes, she told herself. Then I'll wake him and we can get to work.

Woofy, Woofy, thought Wu Fang. I'll never train him to call me by my right name. She had submitted to "Woofy" with reluctance at first, until he had taken her home with him to Upper Montclair three years ago, and she had been pleased with how easily she had been accepted as "Woofy, Taylor's Asian girlfriend with the beautiful long black hair." In China now she wore her hair in a braid, which she pinned around her head like a halo, particularly on the days she instructed her first year English classes. The strict hairstyle made her feel more serious and sophisticated, like a true teacher. When friends asked why she did not cut her hair, she eloquently declaimed her views on what she called "the castration of women in the workplace to suit the convenience of males."

Taylor believed she kept her hair long because he liked it that way, particularly when they made love and she let down her hair and tickled him all over, stroking him with it. He loved her doing that and would pull her down on him, caressing her and nibbling at her face and ears with an energy and excitement he seldom bothered to exhibit elsewhere in their daily lives. "Oh, you're so <u>macho</u>!" she would murmur into his ear. He adored her calling him macho, or even "jock." Either of these words applied to him curved the corners of his mouth into a grin.

But as for her long hair, Taylor was due for a shock. Observing the neat, pixie-like haircuts of many of her girl students, Wu Fang had lately begun to feel a bit old-fashioned with the thick braid that circled her head. She had already made an appointment for this coming Friday with a local hair stylist just off campus to give her a "fashionable" cut. Oh, he'd be surprised!

These days, here at Shi Tong University, the foreigners - she still thought of native Westerners as foreigners, even though she was a U.S. citizen, - called Taylor and her The Bestial Twins, because they teased and baited some of the other young teachers and some of the European foreign students in the dining room. She felt clever tricking the Swedish students, and embarrassing the young French instructor.

It was so amusing to fool naïve people! Taylor's WASP friends in Philadelphia used to say she had mixed Chinese and American Indian blood in her veins, so she was a very international person.

Chapter 6
But Restaurant Food Is Better

Shelby looked through the bright streams of sunlight through her window over to the clock on the wall. It was twenty-five minutes after eleven. The student Li Jian had promised to be at her flat no later than eleven o'clock. It was not like him to be late. What could have happened?

She went into the kitchen. Hungry, she opened the refrigerator and began to take out the bowl of tuna fish salad left over from last night's supper. She savored the salad she was able to make occasionally from tins sent to her from the "care" packages from her family in the U.S. A jar of mayonnaise was precious. She had also found some real celery one day in the local market. It was small and green, but it was celery. Local spring onions were plentiful, and one of those added to the salad made the whole a taste of home that, despite her satisfaction with Chinese food, she sometimes had a desire for.

But, as she was invited out to lunch, she shouldn't at any rate eat anything now. Li Jian would be disappointed if she wasn't hungry when they got to the restaurant. How he loved the ritual of ordering delicious food, putting portions into her bowl, and watching her enjoy them! He'd pour beer slowly into her glass so it did not foam up too much, give himself a full glass afterwards, then make a toast. "To my guest, my teacher."

"Once my teacher, always my teacher," he would say. "To the respected *Laoshi*." He insisted she taste the first bite he would offer her from one of the delicious dishes he had selected. Politely, before tasting any food, she would pick, say, a beautiful steaming prawn from its dish with her chopsticks, and place it in his bowl. This, she learned, was Chinese courtesy.

"Thank you." He would peel the celluloid skin away but, before eating it, pick his chopsticks up to serve her a succulent mushroom from a central dish on the table. She would savor the marvelous scent of sesame as she bit into it. Only after a few turns at this theatrical culinary performance would they begin to eat seriously, helping themselves with spoons or chopsticks to the array of chicken, spiced bean curd, and sesame noodles the waiter had brought.

Shelby felt fortunate in being acquainted with Li Jian. Not only was he an excellent student in her nineteenth century English literature class, he was teaching <u>her</u> so much about China. She thought him a quite sophisticated young man for his twenty-odd years. She hadn't asked him his exact age, although she had learned that inquiring about another's age was common practice in China, that, and asking how much money someone made. She giggled to herself as she thought of how such questions would go over in the States, as casual conversation. "How do you do? And how much money do you make?"

"Hah!" she said aloud.

It was interesting how customs differ so widely in their different cultures. Occasionally, the foreign teacher and Chinese student laughed over what Shelby had come to call the "three refusals of the Chinese politeness." When she had first invited some students to her flat for tea and cookies, she had been disappointed at their initial adamant refusal to touch what was offered them. Only after she had insisted several times had they finally begun to eat the cookies she had baked for them that morning. Later, when the students were on more familiar terms with their teacher, they had explained to her that she should not be offended at their initial refusals to partake of her food and hospitality. It was a Chinese custom to refuse a host's offering three times. Only then should they accept what had been prepared for them. Some students told the story of a classmate who had gone to the U.S. and been offered a delicious slice of chocolate cake by her hostess. When the girl said, "No, thank you" the first time, the hostess replied, "Oh, I'm sorry. I guess you don't eat chocolate," and, much to the girl's chagrin, had taken the lovely cake away. And the student had really wanted it! She was just following Chinese custom.

Now, when something was refused, Shelby simply asked, "Are you being Chinese-polite?" This question had become an enjoyable in-joke among her students.

The ring of the telephone interrupted her daydream of exotic food.

Li Jian was in the lobby. "I'm waiting for you here, *Laoshi*."

Shelby quickly gathered up her gloves and her anorak, which she slung over her shoulder as she went out the door and headed down the stairs. There was Li Jian, in a heavy light blue snow jacket, and wearing a black and white baseball cap, with the visor of course turned backwards, in fashion. As he turned his head, pointing to it for her to admire the cap, she saw imprinted above the visor, *Pittsburgh Steelers*.

"My uncle sent it to me from the States," he said, his tone of voice clearly expressing pride not only in the cap but in his ability to use "the States" as a term he was quite familiar with. His wide grin showed up a set of good white teeth.

From the lobby, Shelby and her student walked rapidly across the quadrangle and out the main gate of the campus, just in time to catch the ponderous public bus heading into town. Several Chinese families, parents toting small children in their arms or on their shoulders, and grandparents carefully holding the hands of brightly-bundled, red-cheeked youngsters in their care, boarded the bus with them. The bus was over- crowded, many riders standing, sardined into the long center aisle, holding onto each other, or where possible, catching at overhead straps.

Li Jian bent to speak to a teenage boy, who swiftly stood up to offer Shelby his place among the seated passengers. Such politeness was difficult to imagine of an American teenager.

"*Xiexie ni*, thank you." She smiled at the young man. Her limited Chinese, articulated in a rich Louisiana drawl, produced a few smiles from other passengers.

When they arrived in the lobby of the White Crane Hotel, they immediately spotted Elaine. She was waiting for them, sprawled in an oversize burgundy sofa framed by the blood-red musty velvet drapes so reminiscent of the colonialism that had economically survived socialist changes.

"Where have you guys been?" Her voice crackled over the lobby. "It's almost one o'clock! I got out of church an hour ago!"

This statement was followed by her equally strident, "Li Jian, you're not going to wear that cap into any lunch with me." The young man looked puzzled for a moment, as Elaine pointed toward his head. Then, smiling, he removed the cap, gesturing as though to hand it to her to admire.

"No, I don't want the thing." She raised her palms and moved back as though about to be attacked by a beast. Shelby, ignoring the typical Elaine-provoked interchange, had started on ahead into the interior of the crowded restaurant.

At their table, Li Jian scanned the menu with his usual enthusiasm, calling for the garlic prawns,

General Chao's chicken, *malatofu*, and a dish of mushrooms and vegetables remembered from a previous lunch Shelby had especially liked. He ordered *qishui*, soda, for Shelby and a beer for himself, Elaine vetoing any drink for herself. Elaine insisted on also ordering for herself. She took from her purse a piece of paper with Chinese characters written on it, which she handed the waiter.

"What's that, Laoshi?" Li Jian inquired.

"My lunch. You'll see."

A few moments later, the waiter reappeared with two slices of white bread on a plate, which he set in front of Elaine. Opening her purse, she took from it a jar of Smucker's strawberry jam and a small penknife. Opening the knife, she began to spread jam on the bread. The waiter meanwhile had placed on the table the other dishes ordered.

With a wave of her hand, Elaine staved off Li Jian's polite efforts to place a prawn on her plate.

"Nuh-uh, none of that stuff for me, thank you. Lord knows what's in it." For almost a year now, she had successfully avoided tasting what she considered to be dirty food. To her uniquely limited knowledge, all of the world's food grown in cultures outside the continental United States was somehow tainted. However, pious blessing prior to eating, which included several makings of the cross over herself, somehow in its mystique absolved certain staples and condiments that, origins notwithstanding, were of Western appearance. This duplicity appeared to absolve them in her mind of the bacteria or poisons she feared. She survived on bread and jam, fruit with skins that could be cut away, and packages from her family in Oregon.

"Li Jian," she said, "Shelby thinks you'll get a scholarship to a university in America next year?"

Li Jian slowly and sedately placed his chopsticks over his bowl before replying.

"My wonderful teacher," he nodded respectfully toward Shelby, "thinks I have a good chance to accomplish this. I am counting on it." He sighed deeply. There are no opportunities here for me. You know very well I may not get the job I want here – it is much better to go abroad."

"You'll be fine," said Shelby, munching a mushroom. She turned toward Elaine. "Li Jian has not only the highest marks in my course, but in the entire Senior class." She smiled at her prize student.

"What about your thesis?" Elaine asked. The senior thesis was written and considered quite separately from class work. The Chinese faculty member in charge of proctoring the senior class oversaw all theses. The final results were handed over to Professor Treadway, the senior English Foreign Expert, in charge of the highly prized two scholarships awarded annually for study abroad at her university.

"I think," said Li Jian with a modest smile that was almost a simper, "my thesis you will find excellent. I have put in unusual effort to make it so. It cannot fail." He placed a crisp chicken wing on his teacher's plate.

"Shelby, aren't you on the scholarship committee? You teach seniors, too," said Elaine.

Shelby put on her brightest smile. "Ah do have some influence," she drawled. She winked at Elaine. "Ah have clout with Stanley."

Li Jian looked intently from one to the other of the two teachers.

He said, "I will die if I do not get the scholarship to America!" He leaned forward in his seat, frowning. "What, please, is 'clout'?"

"Power, man. Power." A dribble of jam ran down the left side of Elaine's lip.
"It's all power ploys." She rattled on, "You know. . .power?"

There was a pause.

"Power ?" Oh, yes, I know about power." Li Jian's eyes were suddenly very bright. "It turns off and on—like the water in the sink, yes? Oh, yes, my grandfather was very powerful after the Revolution. He was on the Long March with Mao Zedong; they were good comrades. You say, 'pals.' But then he was sent to a Gang of Four prison, anyway." The student reached with his chopsticks for a large prawn, which he lifted out of the sauce, popped into his mouth unabashedly, then chewed with open mouth and took a large swallow of beer while he continued to talk excitedly. "Yes, he was very powerful—but he had to go feed the pigs and clean the *cesuo* as though he were NOBODY, nothing!"

As he talked, blood suffused his face, turning it a dark red. Shelby wasn't certain whether it was emotion that was causing that deep blush, or the most of the large bottle of beer he had managed to put away in the past fifteen minutes.

In her short time here in China, Shelby had noticed that the faces of Chinese men turned red when they drank alcohol a lot faster than those of their American brothers. Except for Louisiana rednecks, of course. She giggled to herself. Do you suppose there were Chinese rednecks? Well, more than likely each country had its share of extremists.

"Grandfather's brother was shot by the Gang of Four for being a revisionist," Li Jian was saying. "My family had a very terrible time. Very terrible."

"But your father and your mother both are, what do you call them? Cod-ders, aren't they?" broke in Elaine. "High level bureaucrats."

Shelby looked at her new friend in admiration. Elaine seemed to pick up quickly all sorts of information.

"Cadres, *Laoshi*," softly corrected Li Jian. He spelled it out, "C-a-d-r-e-s. I believe it is originally a French word. Many of our great revolutionaries studied in Europe in the twenties, including my grandfather. Yes," he went back to describing the Li's family trials, "today my family has regained respect, yes. But they were deprived many times," he waved his chopsticks over the table to drive home the point. "Ah, I know something about power, *Laoshi*. But now things are better, thanks to you, my teachers!" Without putting the chopsticks down, he picked up his glass of beer, curling his thumb over the front of the glass while the chopsticks nestled between his hand and the back of the glass.

"*GANBEI!* Bottoms up, my teachers, to you!"

"To your family!" Shelby raised her glass of *qishui* to the toast. Elaine picked up the empty glass beside her plate and clinked it against Li Jian's. In one long draught, he emptied his glass and set it back on the table. He regarded Elaine.

"If you can help me, Professor-"

"I am not a professor, Li Jian. I am one of your masses." She wiped her chin with a napkin. "But we all have clout." She made a fist, not the less metaphorical for the streak of jam on it. "Power. Power! The masses have power. Jesus will help you."

The discussion that followed took them through the end of the meal, Li Jian repeating his confidence that he would succeed. Not only was making his success certain by his own efforts, he praised the help of his foreign teachers. With their encouragement, he would do whatever must be done. His gratitude, and that of his family, would have no bounds. They would be forever in the debt of his benefactors.

Shelby was surprised to find herself thinking that in spite of Li Jian's artless confidences, there was something about him, something she had not noticed before today and that she didn't quite trust. Unaware of any imperfection in his ploys, Li Jian smiled ingratiatingly, and lighted a cigarette as Shelby paid the waitress for their lunches.

Chapter 7
Canteen Food Is Good For You

This noon, the Foreigners' Dining Room reeked of cabbage and turnips, northeast China's favored cold weather vegetables. As Stanley Poussaint entered and walked toward the tables, he unzipped the heavy ski jacket he had already begun to wear although it was only late October. He shivered lightly, aware of the sharp chill in the air, despite a *plink* coming from one of the radiators. Looking around the dining room, he saw that few empty seats were left at any of the dozen big, round tables. Although there was no mandated seating, by tacit mutual consent the Japanese foreign experts and teachers gathered daily at one table at a far right corner of the room; the Russians, at its counterpart on the left side. The English-speaking contingent regularly occupied a long rectangular table along the windows. The remaining tables were filled at will by the variety of foreign students at the University, there to study Chinese language and literature. Now six weeks into the academic term, these represented a cross-section of the world's population, ranging from two Zimbabweans, through Canadians, French, a dozen students from the U.S., others from Japan, Germany, Russia and the Ukraine, Italy, Korea, even a young man from New Zealand. Occasionally, one of the foreign experts or a young teacher would sit for a meal at one of the students' tables. The students, especially the Asian ones, did not as a rule join a table where faculty members were seated, unless specifically invited. When any did, Stanley reflected, they appeared on their best behavior, stiff, resorting to the sort of respect and politeness toward their mentors that was expected in a Chinese classroom.

Stanley found an empty place between Shelby and Taylor, hung his jacket on the back of the chair and sat to wait for the *fuwuyuan* to bring his food from one of the steel serving carts being rolled about the dining hall. He hoped the food would not have gotten too cold again today. The big open pans of food were brought out of the kitchen promptly at noon and, by quarter past, were likely to be at room temperature. Cool, greasy pork lying in a bed of overcooked cabbage and tepid scrambled egg was not a lunch to be looked forward to, but he was ravenous after two lectures during the morning. Yes, the plate set in front of him looked as he had expected it would. But, ah! a hint of steam rose from the bowl of rice set down for him.

No one especially greeted him as he sat down, although Shelby looked up at his arrival, flashing her usual impish grin. As he stretched his legs under the table, his foot accidentally bumped Shelby's.

He said waggishly, "Pardon my roving foot."

Never one to miss a chance for repartee, Shelby shot back, "I'd prefer a roving hand, but a foot will do."

With his chopsticks, he lifted a piece of pork from its dish onto the rice, mashed it down lightly until some rice clung to the meat, then, put the sushi-looking combination into his mouth. He did the same with a piece of the cabbage. A peculiar way to eat, he figured to himself, but at least he was able to put some of the warmth of the rice into his mouth.

As he ate, he listened to Judith at the farther side of the table, her voice raised in some kind of cross-table discussion that he was unable to catch the drift of. Must be serious though, he thought. He seldom heard Judith raise her voice. She struck him always as a laid-back person, considerate of others' feelings, on the whole quite non-judgmental. It would seem to take a fair amount of effort to provoke her.

But if anyone could provoke her, he supposed it would be Taylor Battle and Wu Fang, his Chinese-American wife, the Bestial Twins, as Shelby had wittily dubbed them.

Right now, more interested in getting some food into his empty stomach than in following the conversation, he nevertheless looked over the table at the Bestial Twins, who were laughing stridently at some remark made presumably by Taylor.

"So when the guy told me, 'I teach ESL'," Taylor was saying, "I shot back at him, 'Well, we ALL do that! What else do you teach?'" He guffawed at his self-styled cleverness. Wu Fang laughed along with him. Taylor grinned at her, pleased apparently with her approval in their game of putting down others.

Two insecure kids, Stanley thought, as he observed them.

Those two were outrageous, he told himself. No one could doubt but they were bonded, in an uncanny way. They fed off each other in a symbiotic intimacy that was more than a marriage called for. Like two small children in cahoots, they seemed to relish playing tricks on others. They'd pretend to be friendly, set up their victim with a compliment or a kind gesture, then proceed to try to destroy the person's presence and self-confidence.

Like their razzing the young French teacher Michel, who today was sitting at the table listening quietly to what was becoming a heated discussion about being a Canadian. During the first few days of the semester, Taylor and Wu Fang had together pried unassertive Michel out of his shell, expressing great interest in Quebec, his native province. They had inquired about his classes, asked whether the students in his course responded well to learning French, sympathized with problems of accent he mentioned some of his students having, and had even gotten him around to talking about the politics of Quebec and its struggle for independence from the rest of Canada.

Michel, who was here without family on a two-year teaching assignment, really seemed to enjoy conversing in English, even though his rich French accent marked him as a non-native English speaker. His grammar and his vocabulary were quite sophisticated. An occasional "*Pahr-don?*" with which he interspersed conversation was understood by everyone at table as a signal to repeat, or restate, some few words he had not caught. But Taylor and his wife, the Bestial Twins, insisted on pointing up Michel's miniscule irregularities in a way that was disquieting to everyone else at the table.

"Hey! Wait a minute, everybody," Wu Fang would say when Michel voiced a question that required repetition or explanation. She had a habit of spreading her hands out over the table as she talked, admonishing everyone else to stop their own conversation, and focus on her. "Let's just make sure that le Michel understands what we're talking about here."

Lately, Judith and Stanley had begun to ignore Wu Fang's pronouncements, continuing their own conversations as though she hadn't spoken. Wasn't it Judith who had remarked that, for Wu Fang, the shortest distance between two conversational points seemed to be a complete circle? Shelby had giggled when Stanley relayed that *mot* to her. She pointed out that it was Wu Fang, who was being "just plain MEAN, pure and simple!" Taylor never initiated the attacks; he just imitated his wife. In Shelby's opinion, Taylor did not have one brain cell to rub against another.

Not that others at the table did not occasionally, if unwittingly, provoke hard feelings at the faculty table. Just the other day at lunch, Stanley himself, without thinking of the effect his words might have on Wu Fang, had asked her why she had just "chopped off" the long hair she had been wearing when she first arrived to teach at the University in the fall.

"Have you decided to be a Manchu, after all, and not a great empress?" he had remarked jokingly.

Judith had added, "You look like a lad who's just had his first haircut, or like Peter Pan." She meant it as a pleasantry. Wu Fang did have an impish, boyish appearance, heavily accentuated now by the recent close cut. But the younger woman had reddened at the attention to her new haircut, and had simply lowered her head as though absorbed in the composition of the bowl and chopsticks at her place at table. Then, as if there had been no distraction, she went back to baiting Michel. She explained a sentence to him, defining each word with dramatic gestures, pointing out that "to the university" was "a prepositional phrase", then driving home the basic definition of a phrase, until Michel's pleasant face began to tighten with tension. You could feel the floor shake from his jiggling his foot under the table. But he was too polite to do anything more than nod his head and mutter, "*Je comprends*" deferentially. The excessive illuminations of Wu Fang, assisted by verbal asides from Taylor, often turned a question of his that required simply a 'yes' or 'no' answer, into a master's thesis, and in Wu Fang's ensuing peroration, made an idiot out of the young Frenchman.

As though Wu Fang's aggressive behavior was not enough by itself, Taylor often laced into Michel with a remark on the naiveté of Quebec trying to stand up against the political odds of the rest of Canada.

"You guys are pretty provincial up there in the northeast," he was heard to sneer the other day.

Michel's cheeks had become red, but he remarked simply, "*Pas du tout,*" and continued stabbing at the mashed potatoes on his plate with his chopsticks.

Just now, Wu Fang was holding forth in a raucous voice. "Wai- -t a minute there! I don't see it that way at all."

As she talked, she waved her chopsticks in the air as though she were conducting a band with a double baton, bringing up the sound of trumpets to the left, tubas to the right.

"Everyone doesn't have the same opinions that you guys have. In fact, are you sure you have any opinions?" Her chopsticks brought in the percussion before they veered to pick up a slice of fried pork, which went into the speaker's mouth.

Stanley put down his own chopsticks and picked up his tea glass and drank some. Leaning close to Shelby, he whispered,

"What are they arguing about?"

Shelby shrugged her shoulders.

"The usual." She seemed unconcerned. She picked at the food on her plate, pushing pieces of sliced cucumber out of the way of the cabbage. She helped herself to a mouthful of rice. Stanley felt himself relaxing in her placidity. He made a small effort to find the thread of the conversation. It appeared to be about teaching methodologies.

"Everyone should have opinions." Wu Fang's chopsticks were now directed pointedly at the unfortunate Taylor, who, however, continued to scoop egg and rice into his mouth, seeming not at all undermined by the argument.

But Judith was speaking heatedly.

"I don't understand, Wu Fang, what you think is to be gained by teaching second-year English students how to use "shit" and "fuck" in everyday conversation. They can learn that kind of vocabulary quickly enough if they go into the streets of New York, an unlikely prospect for most of these kids. But I can't see such language appearing on the College Board's Tests of English as a Foreign Language." The TOEFL exam was studied widely throughout China. A successful mark was prerequisite to a foreign student's admission to every U.S. college or university.

"Fuck the College Board," retorted Wu Fang, practically yelling. "They have about as much sense of how people actually talk as you people do."

Judith took a sip from her glass of tea.

"Woofy, don't you think you are being a little carried away? After all, Shi Da didn't bring you all the way out here just to spread the English vernacular to China."

Wu Fang bridled. Since a foreigners' get-together sponsored by the Waiban two years ago, her private nickname, "Woofy", seemed to have made the rounds of the community. Taylor had been a little drunk when he began chasing her around the table at the party that night, calling out, "Woofy! Woofy, darling!" Everyone thought that was very funny.

A little drunk herself, as Wu Fang later told Shelby, who of course passed on the little story to Stanley, it was her opinion their exhibitionism that night was an adroit display of what sophisticated partying WASPS she and Taylor could be. Later, however, cold, sober, she had been horrified at her own un-Chinese behavior. She was, after all, a Chinese-American woman, with great self-respect. It was all right for her husband to call her Woofy, but it was not all right for the others to call her by that name. It was a totally private nickname, and Judith was only trying to abuse her by using it.

Now a mean expression crossed Wu Fang's face. Tensed muscles in her neck stood out. She leaned forward, almost tipping her stool.

"Don't call me Woofy!" she yelled across the table. "Chinese-American women are not called Woofy!" Her face was beet red. "My name is Wu Fang and I'm proud of it!"

"I'm very sorry, Wu Fang." Judith looked very contrite. She leaned forward toward the younger woman in a compassionate gesture. But despite her dignity, she appeared nervous. Stanley wondered what conversation had preceded his arrival at lunch to make Wu Fang look at the older woman with such rancor. He looked around the table for some clue, but everyone was eating silently, with a kind of agreed-upon group concentration, except for Wu Fang, who continued to focus a hostile stare across the table at Judith. Stanley felt Judith stiffen. Wu Fang's disdainful expression translated to irrational dislike. He wondered whether she intended that, or was unaware of the force of her stare.

Meanwhile, Michel, eyes downcast, was frowning, head lowered as he sipped his tea. His expression implied he was participating in a difficult beverage identification contest. Stanley watched him look furtively around the dining room, as though he wished he were at another table. Alone among the foreign teachers, Michel seemed to change tables with each meal these days. Stanley thought of starting up a conversation with him. He looked at his watch, however, and reminded himself that he had an appointment at one. He turned to Michel.

"*Sois sage, mon vieux.* Be good." Stanley stood up from the table, and began putting on his greatcoat. As he did so, he winked amiably at the younger man, who surprised him by giving him a thumb-up gesture of the hand. "*Au revoir, docteur!*"

Stanley reminded himself that he needed to find Elaine to discuss their joint Introduction to English Literature examination that was scheduled for the coming Friday. Of course she was not at lunch.

She seldom came to the dining room, although she occasionally forced herself to join the others in what she claimed for herself was an act of penitence. One should not refuse heathen food when so much of the world was starving to death, she had been heard to remark. Elaine's own dietary habits were beyond his analysis, or interest, for that matter, but he did have to find her for an agreement on their scheduling. "Do you think Elaine is up in her apartment?" he asked Shelby.

"No, she stayed over in her office. She said it was too flubbing cold to walk all the way across the campus and back."

Stanley considered telephoning over to Xin Lou, but quickly decided against it. He had left his cell phone in his apartment. Parts of the internal telephone system were hazardous to one's health, if one had any nerves at all. Some loud phones crackled and buzzed, so that it was almost impossible to hear the person on the other end of the receiver, even if you were lucky enough to get your own party in the first half dozen tries. No wonder most everyone who could afford to do so carried a cell phone these days. Stanley himself owned one, but refused on principle to carry it daily, using the mechanism only when performing his quasi-diplomat functions with the US Embassy, or other related activities.

With a nod to those still at the table and a smile to himself at the bumptiousness of the Bestial Twins, who now seemed to be trying to churn up an argument about "China's criminal elements," Stanley went back out into the cold air, and rode off on his bicycle across campus to Elaine's office.

Chapter 8
Wu Fang Borrows Some Flour

Back at the desk in her apartment, Judith upended the stack of mail she had retrieved from her pigeonhole in the English Department office earlier that morning. There was a mix of envelopes and mail wrappers. Nothing from the States, she noted. It all looked local, a letter or two bearing the beautiful Chinese stamps her eleven-year-old nephew so enjoyed Judith's saving and sending to him. With her letter opener, she carefully slit through the flaps of several envelopes, one after the other. Laying the pile of envelopes to her left, she extracted the letter or advertisement from each one, tossing the unwanted solicitations into the wastebasket. Even in China, she reflected, she was not safe from junk mail. How had she managed to be on so many mailing lists? Besides the usual notices of advertising products she was in neither mood nor money to care about, there was a plethora of announcements of local commercial ventures from Guangzhou, Beijing, and Hong Kong. Joint Sino-U.S. businesses beckoned her with furs, ivory, straw and textile products. A Shanghai firm offered her a choice of catalogue purchases from Peru, New Zealand, or France. She went through the stack of mail quickly, discarding most of it. Ah, a letter from Aunt Olivia, from the States. She had missed that one among all the colorful ads and envelopes.

She put the letter to the side, together with the envelope with its return address in the upper left hand corner. She would need that when she came to reply to dear old Auntie, her mother's elder sister, now in her eighties and planning to visit Judith in China come spring. A note from cousin Kate followed another advertisement. A folded handwritten note in an envelope that looked local was next in the pile. She unfolded it. The handwriting was small with neat cursive script, written with black ink on lined notebook paper. She began to read:

"My darling,

"I don't know how to say—"

A knock sounded at the door.

Laying the letter down, Judith rose from her desk, and crossed the room. The knock had been light, tentative. She hoped it was not a student come shyly to chat, or to ask a favor. She loved her students, and if she did not encourage them to call on her in her rare hours at home during the daytime, she nevertheless willingly respected the need for courtesy when they did. That included inviting the caller in, observing the niceties of asking and being asked after one's health and that of one's family members, and answering politely-put questions on how she was enjoying China. Meanwhile, she had to wait for the student's hesitantly-uttered request to answer a question, borrow a book, or judge a student's competition certain to be held the following evening.

Invariably, the caller felt it a requisite of the visit to give some attention to the several scrolls on the walls, to remark on the professor's good taste in calligraphy, inquiring as well as to as to whether Professor Treadway could read the characters, and offering to read them for her. She had learned to demur to the latter offer, her acknowledgment that she understood the inscription giving her an undeserved reputation for the interpretation of arcane characters. It seemed not to occur to the students that she would long ago have had translated by a professional the fine Chinese handiwork she had from time to time been fortunate enough to purchase or receive as a gift.

"Hello," she said, opening the door to find Wu Fang in the hallway. Wu Fang was proffering a glass cup by its handle, while she pursed her face in an expression meant to express a demure contriteness.

"I'm terribly sorry to bother you, Judith." To her credit, thought Judith, she seldom did. She tried not to show surprise at her visitor. Although the young couple lived in the same foreign teachers' building, their voluntary communication with Judith was as rare as if they shared living in the same apartment building in Manhattan. Wu Fang was smiling in an obvious effort at friendliness.

"I'm really, really sorry, but Shelby's not at home, and I'm desperate for some flour for the *xiaobing* buns I'm making for lunch."

"No problem, Wu Fang." Judith was gracious. "Please do come in." She took the measuring cup from the young woman's outstretched hand, and turned with it into the small kitchen.

"Excuse me, this will take a minute," she called out to the living room. "Sit down. Make yourself at home."

Getting to the cupboard over the refrigerator required her to close the door of the miniscule kitchen. She reached up for the canister of flour among her supplies on the shelf. She set it on the counter and lifted off the top. Using a tablespoon, she filled the measuring cup neatly to the line, and wiped the sides clean with a tea towel, which she replaced on the rack. She picked up the cup, and, opening the door, returned to the living room.

"Here you are."

For a moment, she thought the room was empty. Wu Fang was not on the divan, nor in either of the living room chairs. To her chagrin, she saw that Wu Fang was standing at her desk at the far side of the room, looking over the mail lying open there.

"Woofy." The name escaped her mouth before she could help herself. "I don't think you should be reading my mail, my dear!" The "my dear", phony as it sounded to her own ears, served to help Judith regain some composure at her irritation over what was a pronounced impingement on good manners.

As Wu Fang turned, Judith saw that her face was a deep red. Her eyes looked unfocused, as she opened, closed, and reopened her mouth as though to speak. But she only stuttered, as she turned slowly to look at Judith.

"Thank you for the flour, Judith," she said and, without another word, the young woman ran out of the room. The door banging behind her could have been the wind.

Judith still held the cup of flour in her hand. Setting it on a nearby table, she walked over to her desk. Looking over the top, she picked up an envelope that had been overturned.

"Oh, my God!" What prompted the expletive was not that the envelope was addressed to

Shi Tong University

English Department

the conventional envelope address form in China, but that the third line read,

To Mr. Taylor Battle

Although written in the English language, the address used the conventional Chinese form, writing first the "unit" of employment, in this case the University, and only finally, on the last line, the name of the individual person receiving the message. A letter to Taylor Battle had been placed in her post office box by mistake. In the moments before Wu Fang's coming to her door, she had opened and begun to read a letter addressed not to herself, but to Taylor! She picked up the lined notepaper sheet again and, guilt notwithstanding, was tempted to read it by the salutation, conscious that she was indeed intruding on someone's privacy. The handwriting was clear and easy to read, the letters carefully shaped, as though great diligence had been exercised in laying out the words:

"My Darling,

I don't know
how to say these things
to you. When we met
yesterday, you did not
seem to be convinced
about the situation. If
we love each other, that
is not a problem. I love
you and you love me, I
know. We are little
people. We are not to
worry like boneheads,
as you say. Our love
will carry us everywhere.

I respect you,
my lord and Master.
Everything you make
the decisions about for
our greatest benefit.
Will your wife refuse
you to go? It is you who

are the decision-maker,
the master."

There was a blur at the end of
the line, as though water, a tear, Judith
suspected, had fallen on the paper at
that point.

Although you
are great (another blur)
to your wife, to us you
are the Supreme great.
With ourselves, you are
HE and I am SHE, is
anything more
important in the world?
It is your resolution.

We must run
into the mountains and
hide ourselves. Or we
can go to the
countryside, my
grandmother lives not
too far but reachable by
most lands. We can
join there, and live
happily with our baby,
or die together. We
must arrange quickly to
find our Eden, my love.

The letter was signed "Your Xiao Mei."

Judith thought for a moment, trying to recall whether there was a Xiao Mei among her students. It was impossible to learn the names of over 100 of one's students, when she counted all of her four classes, although she tried hard to get to know as many as possible. She reached into her desk drawer for her register of students. Yes, there was a Wang Xiao Mei in the junior literature class. Judith tried to place the girl in her mind. Yes, she sat in the third row of the English literature lecture. She had fainted one day in class not too long ago, and had to be helped out by some classmates.

Judith reflected that she had already managed student conferences with about half that class. Was this young lady among those scheduled for this week's sessions? She'd have to check her appointment book in the office. Meanwhile, and, at any rate, it was important that this letter be transmitted to its proper recipient without delay. She would have to explain how it had fallen into her hands. She hoped Taylor would not be too upset at her entirely inadvertent induction into what was certain to become, at the very least, a heavy domestic squabble. The letter sounded as though the naïve young girl student, Xiao Mei, had a big crush on her teacher. That was not uncommon. It had to be dealt with in the most sophisticated societies. But it was unfortunate that Wu Fang should find out about it like this. She was a hotheaded little number. Woofy was capable of great histrionics.

Judith felt this matter was hardly one the couple would care to share. She wondered whether she should tell Taylor privately, when she gave the letter to him, that his wife apparently had read it. Oh, dear, what a mess a little carelessness in the office mail distribution system could lead to!

She began to re-fold the letter, preparatory to putting it into her briefcase. She looked at her watch. I'll take the letter to the office this afternoon after lunch, she thought, knowing that Taylor had an afternoon class. She could give the letter to him then, and explain how she had happened to have it. Otherwise, she would simply have to chance placing it in the pigeonhole next to hers marked, "T. Battle." That didn't seem to her a quite honest way to get out of this situation. Besides, how much of the letter had Wu Fang read? How much did she know? Which of the two picked up the mail from the box?

Oh dear, she thought, I have enough on my plate without the intrusion of what looks like the start of the young Battle's marital problems.

There was a knock on at the door. Judith crossed the room and opened it.

Wu Fang stood in the doorway. She held out her hand. She said coldly, "Give it to me."

"Pardon me?" For a second, Judith was taken aback.

Wu Fang extended her hand palm upward and repeated as though speaking to a small child who has pilfered from the candy dish, "I said, give it to me. Give me my husband's letter."

Judith tried to smile, but found herself embarrassed. She turned and walked toward her desk. Wu Fang was right behind her. She was breathing excitedly.

"Did Taylor give this to you?" She snapped her fingers at Judith as though coaxing an answer out of a reluctant witness.

"No, Woofy." She cringed as she heard herself using the name she knew the younger woman hated. "An envelope addressed to Taylor was placed in my mailbox by mistake." Judith still held the letter, hesitating. After all, it was addressed to Taylor. But Wu Fang was not to be denied.

"Give it to me!" Her face was blotched deep red.

When she had left, Judith realized that the envelope in which the letter had been posted was still lying on her desk.

Chapter 9
Plagiarism or Carelessness?

Li Jian took one final puff on the Black Star cigarette in his hand. Flicking thumb against forefinger, he tossed it to the floor of the corridor. He rapped three times on the door of the third office in Xin Lou marked "Foreign Experts Office."

His foreign English professor's voice called, "*Jinlai.*" Come in."

He suppressed a smile at the teacher's Chinese accent. Why did foreigners have such trouble pronouncing Chinese with the correct tones? Sometimes what they said turned out to be not at all what they meant. They'd say, "*Ba yen gei wo,*" "give me some salt," for example, when they meant to say the "Ba yen *gei yen*" with a flat tone that meant "Give me a cigarette!" Most of the time what they said was unintelligible.

"Good afternoon, Li Jian. How are you?" Professor Treadway motioned with the pen in her hand toward the chair beside her desk. "Please be seated."

He sat wordlessly, running his eyes over the papers on the wide, wooden surface to see whether he could spot his own.

He watched the professor take from the pile and open the blue manila folder he had lovingly made for his presentation and glance through several of the pages. She didn't even seem to bother about the beautiful calligraphy on the cover for the title of his thesis. He had even added the date and her name, Professor Judith Treadway, below his own name, in perfect Western cursive script.

While she leafed the document and he waited for her to begin talking, he glanced around the office. The other desk in the room belonged to Teacher Johnson, he knew. Its top was bare except for a bowl with some red plastic flowers in it and a quite large book propped up beside the flower arrangement. By turning his head more to the left and leaning forward, he could spell out the title: Webster's Tenth Collegiate Dictionary.

"Li Jian," the professor was saying, "I read your paper with great interest."

He looked at her expectantly. He felt in the breast pocket of his jacket for his cigarettes, but caught himself in time and returned his arm to the side of her desk on which he had been leaning. He was doing his best to keep as calm as possible.

"It's quite well done."

"Thank you, Professor." His look was that of the very serious student who would not permit himself to smile for fear that the action would seem immodest. Chinese dignity should not allow the face to show too great pleasure. That would come later, when he was alone.

"You show a surprising grasp of semantics." Professor Treadway hesitated a moment, as she leafed through several pages. "I had no idea during our conferences on your choice of subject matter that you would go into such depth in your paper. I had expected a general exploration of the science of linguistics. . ." Her voice trailed off as she continued to riffle through his paper.

"Thank you. You are too kind."

"This shows great capability."

"Oh, no, no." His right hand made a self-deprecating gesture.

"Yes, it's quite excellent!" She had gotten to the end of the paper now, and was looking at the last page.

"You've forgotten to put in your bibliography." Professor Treadway seemed not unduly surprised. Some of her brightest students suffered academic blindness as far as correct research attributions were concerned.

He moved his head nearer the desk, as though to look at the paper with her. He said nothing.

"Where is your bibliography?" She looked directly at him.

"Yes, yes. I forgot." He reached for the paper. "I will put the bibliography."

Her hand remained on the paper.

"You can bring it to me tomorrow. By the way, what Korzibski did you read?"

"Pardon me, Professor?"

"Li Jian, you know about footnotes. But you have none here in the paper. I'm afraid that is unsatisfactory. Which text of Professor Korzibski are you quoting here?" She flipped through his paper to another page, which, like each of the others, was unmarred by any corroborative evidence of source.

"'Sentence articulations of common knowledge,'" she read, "are more easily treated as synthetic propositions." She ran a finger along the lines of his handwriting as she read, ". . .and frequently provide a vital part of the residual analogy that the metaphor tries to convey." She tapped the paragraph with her finger, as though chiding its obliqueness.

"Yes." Li Jian said simply.

"A very interesting idea. You attribute it to Korzibski, but do not credit the source. Also, it's a good idea to redefine some of this material in your own words." She paused, flipping through the paper again. She seemed to be smiling. That was a good sign.

"Did anyone help you with this paper, Benjamin?"

He liked it when she used his English name, which she seldom did. He had written, "A Study of Hidden Meanings in Certain Intransitive Verbs, by Benjamin Li" on the outside cover of his thesis, and only below in the calligraphy the 'Benjamin' in parentheses and small letters had he added ('Li Jian'). She'd better get used to calling him Benjamin, because that was the name he was going to use when he went to America. He thought he'd probably change the 'Li' to 'Lee', too. A friend of his who had been to

California said there were many Lee families there. Also, he had even seen in a slide in his TOEFL class some American cakes made by a famous woman called Sarah Lee. He was going to be famous, too, though not for making cakes.

He looked at Professor Treadway ingratiatingly, touching an outstretched hand to his forehead, palm downward, in a gesture of respect.

"Only your good teachings, Professor."

"Well, thank you. But I didn't really teach you all of this." She was still smiling.

The young man was not to be put off. "But you taught us research, Professor."

He made a further effort to reach for the paper, but she continued to hold it firmly under her hand.

"What is my grade?"

A tap sounded at the door.

Professor Treadway folded her hands over his paper.

"Li Jian, if you will bring your bibliography and footnotes to me tomorrow, we shall be able to discuss this more thoroughly. Now I'm afraid your time is up." She looked at her watch. He continued to sit, his mouth open to speak.

"Another student is waiting," Professor Treadway said, nodding toward the doorway.

Flashing as wide a smile as he could muster, Li Jian rose and left the office, passing the student Song Ming on her way in.

Song Ming was one of those shy, traditional Chinese young ladies whose modesty overcame any apparent need for her to speak up or defend any statement she might actually be bold enough to make. In class, she spoke, when at all, in a light whisper, as though burdened with chronic laryngitis. How she had gotten to be a graduate student, or, "post graduate", as they were called in China, was a mystery. Her work was mediocre, at best. She plodded through her classes, turned in all her work on time, although the work was as spineless and unimaginative as the girl herself. But it was thorough, and conscientious. Professor Treadway looked through a paper of hers now. Of the five graduate students in her course in literary criticism, Song Ming was one she could be certain never dared think an individual thought, let alone utter it aloud. Practically every statement in the written work cited an authoritative source. She had chosen international metaphors in "Leaves of Grass" as the subject of her research paper and even the birth date of the poems' author, Walt Whitman, had been substantiated by a footnote, "1819-1892, cf. Professor Edwin H. Miller," one of Whitman's biographers, as well as the fact that "the work contains twelve untitled poems, proceeded by a preface." For Song Ming the concept of public domain simply failed to exist. So fearful was she of "stealing" someone else's ideas, her papers were pockmarked with footnotes. A suggestion of cutting out some of them sent a shiver through the girl's body, as though she were being asked to commit an evil deed.

Judith was glad when the fifteen-minute period was up, and the next student waiting for a conference knocked. It was becoming a long, rather tedious afternoon.

Bhong Taur was next. Following a light knock, he poked his head deferentially around the door and offered his broad smile. "May I come in?"

"Good afternoon, Bhong Taur." She motioned him to sit in the chair beside her desk. "How is your good mother the librarian these days?"

Bhong Taur did not miss the point. He grinned. "You are kind to ask, *Laoshi*! She is very well, thank you. And very busy!" He added. She noted that he used the generic word for teacher, *Laoshi*, always, when he addressed her, unlike many of the English majors in her class who prided themselves on using the English nomenclature "Professor."

Professor Treadway had been surprised to learn from Chairman Zhang just a week or so ago that her very intelligent minority senior student Bhong Taur was from a unique background. He came from a village in the mountains that had a curious success story. Six years ago, an American newspaper reporter had written a feature story about Bhong Taur's hometown, pointing up certain rudimentary conditions of village life including the fact that no books were available in the local school except basic textbooks. (That this was a fact in thousands of villages was not mentioned in the article.) A Chicago businessman, on reading the story, had opted to decrease his own income tax by donating several thousand dollars to the construction of a library in the village. It was of course to bear his name. Bhong Taur's mother, a primary school teacher, was today the head librarian of the Alfred McGee Library of Tao Shan village. She with pride and deference accepted her son's suggestions for literary works in English for the library, for which Benefactor McGee allocated a modest but tidy budget. Bhong Taur's village thus possessed the only library in rural China to retain copies of W. H. Auden, Henry James, and William Saroyan, authors whom Bhong Taur had taken special liking to during his university years, and a list of whose works he proudly sent to his mother.

In this, his senior year at Shi Tong, Bhong Taur had blossomed. Over the past four years, he had shed his initial diffidence as an artless country lad, to become one of the most active and responsive students in his class. His senior thesis, a comparison of the poetic techniques of Robert Lowell and Theodore Roethke, was exceptionally, and painstakingly, well done.

If his mid-term exams passed muster, and she had no reason to think they would not ~ he was proving able and conscientious in every academic task ~ he probably also stood a good chance of being a candidate for a coveted Mohegan exchange scholarship. That he was of a minority group from northeast China and not of Han descent might not sit well with some of her more conservative Chinese colleagues in the Department. But that would do him no harm once he got to America. And, wouldn't the librarian of Tao Shan village be a proud mother!

She had divulged none of these thoughts yet to Bhong Taur, who sat attentively in the chair beside her desk as she went over his paper and suggested a few emendations.

"I agree, *Laoshi*, that I should perhaps have more examples of this rhyme scheme. But I was not able to find any copies of the volume of *Open House*, or even of *The Waking*. Only the title poems are in the Norton Anthology."

Judith was quite aware of the limitations of the University library, particularly in the matter of contemporary literature. Nor was she unaware of the irony of the American millionaire's hefty gift to a tiny village while a major state university went intellectually hungry. Although acquisitions had quintupled in the ten years she had been coming here, the collection of twentieth century literature was still at minimum. She herself owned a significant collection she had managed to transport to China over the years. These books she willingly loaned when she was in China, to enthusiastic, knowledge-hungry students, but had the University store them for her along with her personal house effects when she returned to the U.S. She liked to be certain they would be available to her new batch of students in the subsequent years as they needed.

Everyone was aware of the official librarian, Heavenly Fountain's protective custodial care of the foreign section of the university library. She treated books as though they were the Hope Diamond, to be viewed only under tight security and supervision.

"I believe I have several volumes of Roethke in my apartment, Bhong Taur. I'll be home this evening if you'd like to come by to borrow what you need."

"Thank you, *Laoshi*," the young man replied. "You are very kind." He shifted his chair. "Thank you also for advising me which poet to use, Theodore Roethke or Robert Lowell?"

Judith hesitated only a second before replying. "That is what you yourself must decide, Bhong Taur. That is one of the purposes in writing your thesis."

"Oh, of course, my dear teacher." He looked at her soberly for a moment before his smooth face broke into a huge smile. "Oh, yes, that is being a scholar, yes? I like to be a scholar! Then one day soon you will let me go to America, yes?" With a swift, slightly obsequious bow, he was gone, before Judith could muster a suitable reply.

With a sign, she turned in her chair to look out of the window. So many students with high expectations!

When the last student had finally left, Judith sat for a few minutes staring out of the window. She appeared to be studying a choir of chickadees harmonizing on the bare branch of a tree nearby. Below her, students moved about the quadrangle in orderly if casual formations, some carrying lunch pails, others their ubiquitous thermos bottles of hot water. The "Pepsi generation" in China, especially among the many students from suburban or rural areas of the country, remained the hot water drinkers their ancestors had been before them. The thermos containers of boiled water were everywhere to be seen. Judith smiled as she recalled Stanley saying many years ago, about the upheaval of the Tiananmen student demonstrations, "Tanks? Grenades? If they had just taken their thermos bottles away from them, they'd have China on its knees!"

She sipped at the tea she had concocted for herself from the use of the small sterno outfit on her desk, a leftover from her camping days, which she had brought from the States. She clasped the mug tightly around to warm herself, as she continued to watch and hear the birds. She found herself listening for a pattern through the double glass of the storm windows. The glass was thin and not really sealed properly. Blasts of drafty wind rippled through the chinks around the sill, creating a kind of ghostly contrapuntal with the chickadee-dee-dee of the birds. She wondered if the activity of chirping helped keep them warm.

The cup of hot tea warmed her hands. The radiator under the window *plinked* once, providing the merest clue that, somewhere in this vast building, a furnace was functioning at minimal level with strenuous activity. She put her hand down to feel its heat. Not much there.

She swiveled around in her chair to face the papers on her desk, the papers that had, in fact, prompted her seeming meditation among the birds for the past fifteen minutes. She had promised herself not to agonize over these student papers. What was she going to do about the problems? She was concerned about Li Jian. Although he was one of the brightest of the seniors, actually, a strong scholarship candidate, she wondered whether he could write as well as this paper indicated. Was he plagiarizing? If so...

Then again, no footnotes. No bibliography. Li Jian could be expected to know better. Her own field was literature. It was usual to call on other experts to read a thesis outside one's own special field. She would ask Professor Poussaint to give the paper a second reading. After all, he was the linguistics expert.

Each year, a few of these senior final efforts were excellent; most were routine to mediocre. She whisked the pile of unread papers, still a good half dozen to go. She had two failures so far, one a piece of illiteracy from a student who had been weak the entire term. When she had asked him one day what the topic of his paper was to be, he had replied, "Yes, ma'am, my mother lives in Qiqihar." How he had managed to become a senior in a reputable university could hardly be guessed at. Well, yes, it could be guessed at. The boy's parents had money and political contacts. He had failed to pass the university entrance examination, but subsequently was able to attend by paying his own way, rather than having the state underwrite his education. The private family resources of substandard students who were fortunate to have affluent parents who were strongly politically connected and had become wealthy under China's current economic progress brought into the university coffers needed funds, but was not at all a step toward increasing the prestige of the university. However, that political party was not her affair.

Her other absolute failure so far was, where was that paper? Its author, a solemn-faced, silent young man who had been transferred into her class during mid term with no explanation other than that he was "to observe the class but be treated and graded like an ordinary student." "Like an ordinary student" meant he was probably some politico's cousin or nephew. He exhibited no intellectual background or prowess besides his ability to copy words direct from the Norton Anthology. He had really mucked up; there was no doubt about it. He had plagiarized almost the entire middle section of his thesis so obviously it was hard to believe. He had lifted an entire chapter out of one of the most common American literature books on the reference shelf. Here it was, word for word. She bent her head to examine closely the spidery handwriting and compare it against the copy of the Norton's Anthology, which lay open on her desk. Not only did he use no quotation marks and give no acknowledgement to the source of the information, but also the student had made no effort to write an original line. True, he was far from the brightest in the class. She had hoped, however, that he could manage to squeak through. Well, he had "squeaked," but not through.

Now she had the unpleasant task of informing him he had no chance of passing her course this term. The fact that he was failing before he attempted the paper confirmed the inevitable. Perhaps he had supporters in the department who would advocate giving him another chance in the time remaining to graduation. Such advocacy was not unknown in the university. Perhaps the boy would be hostile and threaten her. Such behavior also was not unheard of. Last year when Professor Du failed a student, the young man had gone to the teacher's house at night, broken a window, and disconnected the faculty member's propane gas tank in the kitchen. Fortunately, a member of the household had smelled the gas almost immediately, so no harm had been done. But it was not the kind of incident one cared to be involved in.

She looked at her watch. Almost six o'clock. She was tired and hungry. She stashed her papers in her briefcase, and headed for the Foreign Experts Building.

Chapter 10
Search and Seize

While Taylor was out of the apartment teaching a class up in Main Building, Wu Fang, with jealousy and anger, dark thoughts of vengeance in her heart, was in their bedroom, systematically going through bureau drawers, and then through the clothes in their big beige wood wardrobe. She would find any evidence there was of Taylor's misconduct.

Taylor's jackets were strewn over the floor. His blazer, with his old school logos, his ski jacket, the gray wool vest he sometimes wore to class, all joined the growing stack she examined with rough pulls and thrusts, then tossed to the floor. She pulled out and attacked his blue suitcoat, checking each pocket, inside and out. She smelled the cloth, sniffing along the linings like a cat tracking a mouse. So far, she had found nothing but the stale smell of cigarettes.

She was about to give up when she spied his plastic raincoat that had fallen to the floor of the closet. He had not worn that since the snows began. As she lifted the coat, she felt something hard against her hand. Reaching into the deep side pocket, she extracted the object. She held it in the palm of her hand and looked at it for a very long time. She began to tremble. A mixture of trepidation and terrible hatred crossed her face. She carefully replaced the clothes on their hangers in the closet.

Chapter 11
The Friday Night Club

The Friday Night Club of English teachers was to meet at Chairman Zhang Jingchun's flat this week, at seven o'clock. His sister had spent the afternoon preparing meat and vegetables for a Mongolian hot pot. Now the table was set, the raw lamb sliced, and vegetables cut just to the proper bite size, surrounded the large copper *huoguozi*, which was filled with a broth and placed in the center, its electric plug dangling at the side of the table, ready to be inserted into the wall socket once the guests were seated. He was glad his sister had insisted on his replacing the old-fashioned hot pot cooker with this new one. The original one Zhang Jingchun remembered fondly from his earliest days of marriage, when it had been presented to the young couple as a wedding gift. After his dear wife had died suddenly, he had not been able to look at it for years without crying. His more practical sister had finally warned him that living alone, he was likely to light the charcoal, which heated the old one and asphyxiate himself through his absentmindedness. She was kind to him. He looked over the food prepared and laid out on a table in his study, a room larger than his tiny kitchen, where he cooked and ate when alone. She must have taken the afternoon off from work to get everything ready early for this evening's bachelor dinner, as the foreigners called it.

In addition to the hot pot ingredients, there were sesame noodles, mushroom noodles and slices of cold beef sausage.

The doorbell sounded. Dr. Zhang went down the tiny hall that led to the doorway, and opened the door to greet the first of his guests. It was Dr. Poussaint, unfailingly punctual.

"Good evening, Stanley." The clock in his small study to which he led his guest was just striking seven.

"Good evening, Jingchun."

"You are more punctual than the Chinese," the Chairman said jovially.

"I detest being late."

"That is very good for your students."

The doorbell sounded again. "Excuse me, please." Dr. Zhang went again to the door. "Ah, my dear friends, so fine to see you, Judith, Elaine, Shelby, come in, my dears, come in." The women each handed him her coat, which he carefully hung in the closet.

"Taylor and Wu Fang begged off for the evening. So, shall we go right to table? You must be starving after such a long, hard day." He led them all down the small corridor to his study, where the table had been set and surrounded by five stools. Shelby admired the hot pot. "Oh, I just love it so! We don't have anythin' LIKE this in Louisiana!"

"Stanley, I will place you opposite me, and let the beautiful women surround us."

Shelby placed herself at Stanley's right elbow. Judith moved to the stool next to Shelby and beside their host. That left the setting on the other side of the round table between the two men free for Elaine.

"To my guests!" Chairman Zhang raised his glass, which, like the others, held the fragrant plum dinner wine, a specialty of Northeast China. "Thank you all for coming to the humble dinner before you." Everyone raised their glasses for the ceremonial toast before beginning the meal.

As they ate, they discussed the upcoming American literature conference in Beijing. Dr. Zhang would not be able to attend, much as he felt he could especially profit from listening to scholars discussing new trends in postmodernist literature. Stanley pleaded indifference to what he termed the "acolytes' ritual." Judith was tied up with the work on the Scholarship Committee.

The dinner was one Dr. Zhang especially liked to serve on social occasions like these, as it meant his sister would prepare the ingredients early, set the cold dishes in the refrigerator and then leave to care for her own family. Mongolian hot pot is a dish individual guests can enjoy making themselves. Everyone dug in, cooling bits and pieces as they wished. Only Elaine, as was her habit, helped herself to nothing but the bowl of peanuts on the table.

The Chairman said, "Elaine, why don't you think of going to the conference? You teach American literature, and I think you would have excellent contributions to make to the meeting. There will be a good number of your countrymen there, I understand."

Elaine made a wry face.

"I'll go if you insist," she replied, "but I hate Beijing. It's too big and too dusty. The only decent thing about Beijing is the bread. They do have good bread."

She picked up another peanut with her chopsticks, and dropped it clinking onto her plate.

Stanley, busy capturing a mushroom from the hot pot with his chopstick, said, "While we're speaking of conferences, what is this poetry meeting coming up soon? The calendar just says '*kaiwei*', which doesn't tell much about what kind of meeting."

"It's a poetry reading and party that's been organized by the Waiban," Dr. Zhang said. He added, "although it's officially a Foreign Languages Department function. This will be its second year. It provides a good stimulus for the foreign literature students and the Chinese literature majors to get together. Of course, all teachers in the Department are invited." He stretched out his open palms before him to emphasize that he meant not only his dinner guests.

"Why do they always have to have a party?" snorted Elaine. "Why can't they just have a serious competition?"

"Oh, a little fun never hurts anyone," Judith said pleasantly. "These kids all work pretty hard."

"Are we expected to perform, too?" Stanley made an ape-like face. He immediately corrected himself by setting his countenance straight in the mock-innocent expression of a small boy caught making a face behind a teacher's back.

"Oh, you love to recite poetry, you know it, Stanley!" laughed Shelby prettily. She swung her long, taffy-colored hair back over her left shoulder as she regarded him.

"Where in the world did you ever get that idea?" he retorted. "I'd rather undergo Chinese water torture!"

"At any rate," Dr. Zhang said amiably, "participation is voluntary. Mostly students and young teachers. I think they're calling it a Poetry Festival. However," he added, "I hope each of you will be able to attend at least a part of it. Some senior teacher interest will be most welcome."

The telephone rang. The Chairman went to answer it.

Elaine watched him as he walked down the corridor.

"That poor man never gets a minute's peace," she said. "I don't know how he stands it living all alone."

"Now, now, Elaine," Dr. Poussaint teased. "He's a little young for you."

"If I want comments from you, I'll ask for them." She threw him a dirty look.

Judith quickly said, "Oh, come off it, Elaine. Stanley's just joking." But she felt a chill as a look of animosity passed from Elaine to herself.

"Just a student." The Chairman had returned to the room. "He wanted to know when the seniors would hear who had won the scholarship."

Elaine said, "They shouldn't be calling you at home about things like that."

The Chairman did not mind. His gentle eyes twinkled. "It's very important to them. I might say it's the most important announcement of the year."

"That's for sure," said Stanley. "Everybody wants to go abroad to study."

"And to have this opportunity to go right after graduation."

"I find myself doubly justifying each single low mark I give these days," Judith sighed. "I never used to feel quite so guilty about giving poor students low grades."

"Well," Stanley interjected, "I don't like to sound like the heavy in the student-faculty drama, but, for better or worse, we're responsible for the kids' toeing the straight and narrow. Especially in these days, when more and more of the world's young seem to think cheating is the way to go. But, do excuse me," he said, slapping a hand against his chest. "It seems I am preaching. Unfortunately, most of our students here will never see a foreign campus." Stanley sipped at his glass of beer, one of which had been placed beside each guest's wine glass, as was the custom.

Their host busied himself refilling the glasses as soon as they had been drunk from, in Chinese courtesy.

"None for me." Elaine put her hand over the glasses at her place.

"Oh. I'm sorry. A little *qishui*, soda pop?" The Chairman looked desolate, that a guest had nothing satisfactory to drink.

"I know what *qishui* is. You don't have to explain. Yes, that'll be fine, please."

"Anyone else?"

"I think," said Judith, "we should announce the scholarship winners as early as we can. We have additional administrative details this year. And it's already quite late."

Elaine was practicing picking up peanuts from her otherwise empty plate.

"Miss Tryst!" said Dr. Zhang, with solicitous alarm. "You have really not eaten anything!" In the manner of a Chinese host, he placed on her plate a slice of the delicious looking *liangpannuro*, sliced spiced beef, one side dish at the dinner.

Elaine winced, and put her hand over her plate.

"No, no. Nothing for me."

"But you must eat."

"I've already eaten my dinner." She made the statement flatly, without apology, as though it were simply a fact of everyday life to have one's dinner before attending a dinner party. The good Chairman looked puzzled.

"E-laine, Miss Tryst, are you all right? Do you feel well?"

"Oh, perfectly well!" It was obvious she did not intend to give any explanation for her behavior. Dr. Zhang tipped his head to the side somewhat in a manner of a curious sandpiper, as he regarded his guest.

Shelby Johnson broke the awkwardness.

"I just haven't had time to finish marking my senior term papers yet, let alone computing their little old grades." With her chopsticks, she fished around in the broth of hot pot for another tantalizing slice of lamb. Elaine had said it was goat meat. Shelby thought it tasted delicious dipped in the peanut sauce beside her plate.

Judith said, "To tell you the truth, I haven't finished either one. I still have a couple of papers I'm not certain about. Well, this weekend I shall have plenty of time."

Dr. Zhang looked at her fondly. "Sometimes we don't have the kind of time we think we have."

As for Judith Treadway, she had no way of knowing that this was the last weekend she would ever have any time at all.

Chapter 12
No Footnotes

It was ten minutes before noon. Li Jian streaked down the steps of Main Building two at a time, like a bullet, he said to himself as he passed on the fringe of the crowds of other students on their more pedestrian ways to lunch. He had gotten up too late for breakfast this morning, and certainly did not feel like bucking the long lines that would be forming in a few minutes. Nor did he want cold food today. As all students knew, the cafeteria workers set the dishes of food for sale out on the counters starting at about quarter to noon. By 12:10 or 12:15, the hot food remaining was stone cold. Some students and university workers who ate here did not seem to mind. They were used to it, but not Li Jian. He wanted hot and fresh! He sprinted, and leapt up the stairs to the door of the dining building.

Aiya! A long line had already snaked toward the still-closed door of the canteen. Li Jian continued running along the length of the queue. Just as the doors were being flung open to let in the mass of waiting students, he spied some of his pals near the front of the lines. Sprinting, he pushed ahead into the dining hall with them. Inside, he and the friends he had joined shoved in front of some women students already at the cafeteria steam table, prompting one demure young lady whom Li Jian elbowed to dig a heel sharply into his instep as she regained her position in front of him

"*Tamada!*" he bleated, stomping his injured foot. Ignoring his cries and wounded looks, the girls quietly, and without a further glance at him, selected their food from among the many small dishes of vegetables on the cafeteria counters, some with a few chicken pieces, tofu, the white bean curd, egg drop soup, and bowls of rice and set off in the direction of the tables. Angry, he began to follow the girl who had kicked him. He decided he would run past her and knock her tray, spilling her food. But his hunger was getting the better of him. Regaining his composure enough to hand over his food vouchers quickly to a counter woman, he picked up two large enamel bowls of rice and a small one of the tofu, and hurried to find a table with his pals.

After eating the meal, sitting over their emptied enamel bowls at one of the big round tables in the center of the canteen, some of his friends lit cigarettes. Li Jian pulled his own pack from his jacket pocket. Extracting two cigarettes from the rather crushed pack, he offered one across the table to his pal, Pao Hu. He dug up some matches from another pocket, and lighted both the cigarettes.

"Pao Hu, ah," he said in a low voice, "Let's you and me get some drinks tonight. I feel like drinking."

The student Pao Hu gave him a dissenting look. "Why tonight? I have class early tomorrow morning."

"I am not happy. I have a little problem." He proceeded to delineate to Pao Hu a very small aspect of his problem, that the senior English professor was not satisfied with some of the footnotes in his most important final term paper.

"But that is easy to repair. What's the matter?"

"Not so easy. I don't want any mistakes in that paper. Why should there be mistakes in it? It should be perfect." He leaned forward toward Pao Hu, flicking ashes onto the table and the dirty bowls and chopsticks that lay around. His voice shook with emotion and nervousness.

"What is the matter?" he squeaked. "The matter? You ask me? The matter is that I must receive one of the scholarships. My heart has been set on it. My family's heart is set on it. I cannot disappoint myself or them! That is final!" He had clenched a fist, as he spoke. Now he banged it down hard on the table, sending a bowl rolling to the floor.

Pao Hu was taken aback at Li Jian's agitation. His classmate's reputation for being the all-knowing, "cool" type was certainly not in evidence here.

"All right. I'll meet you tonight. Let's have some beers. I have money today. I will buy several bottles after class." He regarded his friend with raised eyebrows, but a kindly expression.

"We will talk about your problem some more tonight, Jian. Perhaps the paper needs no footnotes."

"Come to my room at seven o'clock." Li Jian was speaking again in an undertone, looking around to see if anyone else was hearing him. The other students at the table had left.

"I will. I must go and check my mailbox now. *Zaijian!*"

Looking at his watch, Pao Hu pushed back his stool, and shot out of the canteen, forgetting to bus his dirty bowl and spoon. Li Jian lighted another cigarette, and sat pondering for a few minutes, puffing smoke in small circles into the air. After a few moments, he picked up the dirty containers and stacked them to carry them away more easily. He carefully placed into his back pocket a metal spoon Pao Hu had been using.

Chapter 13
Heavenly Fountain Guards the Library

Heavenly Fountain walked through the stacks that held the rows of neat, carefully catalogued volumes like a general reviewing her troops. Nothing was out of line in these stacks of books that she examined with a careful eye for any minute flaw the sterile air of the room might have inflicted during the night. Red, grey, green-bound volumes, thick tomes and slender monographs, were catalogued and arranged with the devotion and perfection for which Heavenly Fountain was herself renowned in her guardianship of the Foreign Book Section of the University Library.

Some of these volumes were very expensive, she knew. She ran her hand along the top of the set of *The Encyclopedia Britannica*, to be certain her well-trained *fuwuyuan* had dusted each book properly. The thirty-two beautiful leather volumes had been donated to the University Library by a foreign educational foundation set up by an American who had made millions selling his rich compatriots automobiles. She let her mind wander briefly in a thought that one day even she might own an automobile! Her sister's husband, the construction engineer, had bought one, and she had ridden in it only last Sunday.

She pulled herself with a start back to the surveillance, her important work. Heavenly Fountain took special pride in the shiny, upright dark red volumes with gold lettering. Sometimes she felt it a pity that all the foreign novels and other literature books could not be the same size and shape, which would give them more of a classical Chinese appearance. Nevertheless, she was quite content with her efforts to organize and preserve these precious cultural documents from the West, treasures entrusted to her keeping.

She continued her daily parade through the stacks. For a Chinese, she was unusually tall. She walked with that lope characteristic of certain tall, large-boned women. Her tallness pleased her. In her work she was able to reach the top shelves of books without the inconvenience of having to carry a stool with her. Now, as she walked the stacks, her eyes missed no aberration, no slight irregularity in the orderly rows of books. Each shelf, high or low, had perfect alignment; she would not be satisfied with less than perfect neatness in the ranks.

Emerging from between two rows, she observed a young man standing in front of her desk, at the railing that separated the book collection from the public. She went on to complete her inspection of the final echelon of stacks, then rounded off the tour back at her desk.

"What is it?" She examined some index cards on her desk, barely glancing at the young man.

"*Tian Laoshi*," the student offered an obsequious bow in her direction, folded hands raised to his forehead. Heavenly Fountain reflected the student must be aware that in these modern times such a serious kowtow was no longer looked upon favorably by the authorities. What was this young man up to?

"Tian *Laoshi*," he repeated. "May I respectfully have a word with you?"

She looked up at him from her desk, but without expression.

He was saying, "I am working on my senior thesis, which is due very shortly."

Her face remained impassive. The student was having some trouble getting his words out. The skin of his face had begun to turn a dark red. But he continued,

"I know we should not ask you for special favors that are not permitted, *Laoshi*. But you are very kind." This reflection appeared to have no effect on the librarian's implacability. Judging from the way she was threading through some of the papers on her desk, she might not even have heard him.

"I need to look at some books for my research."

"What class are you?"

"Class four, senior, Laoshi."

Heavenly Fountain consulted a calendar on her desk. She riffled through several pages before she found the notation she was looking for. She said, "Class Four's time to come to this library is Tuesday morning at third period, ten o'clock."

"I was unable to come on Tuesday morning."

"You may come with your class next Tuesday morning."

"That will be too late, *Laoshi*. Please." He leaned over the desk toward her, and was whispering, "I must complete my paper this week." He glanced from side to side. No other students were in the library.

Heavenly Fountain's attention was drawn to a speck of dust on her desk. She pulled a rag from a desk drawer and began to tap noisily at the desk.

"Please let me use some books, even if it is not in the regulations. It is very important."

The student's pleading with his eyes was lost on Heavenly Fountain.

"The regulations do not permit it," she replied curtly. "Come next Tuesday."

"But it will be too late!"

"I cannot break the law."

The student took from his book bag a notebook. Laying the book bag on the floor, he opened the notebook to a page of scrawls. He pointed, "Here, please, this one. Could I just have a look at this one book?" His tone was imploring.

"You are not permitted to use this room except on Tuesday mornings." Heavenly Fountain heaved a heavy sigh of impatience with the young man who refused to understand necessary library procedures.

"May I just sit to look at a book here for a few minutes, to help me to answer some questions?"

"I cannot leave my desk." The librarian had seated herself at her desk, hands folded in front of her.

"I could get it myself, to spare you." His hand motioned toward the stacks. "I would be most careful."

"You know that is not allowed."

During Li Jian's final pleas, the eyes of Heavenly Fountain had been directed to a spot in space somewhere above and behind Li Jian's left ear. Now she redirected her attention to a few library cards in the center of her desk and with concentration began to record on a master sheet three books that had been taken out during the course of the day, together with the names and identification numbers of each of the lucky borrowers.

Chapter 14
A Disgraceful Deed is Uncovered

"I've had it. I can't take any more."

It was a Friday night. Stanley was leaning back comfortably on Judith's big Foreign Affairs Office-issue sofa. The furniture in the foreign experts' apartments had been specially ordered from Japan, Stanley knew, a great concession to foreign taste. Trouble was, it looked and felt as though it had all been made for little people, and probably was. The couch on which Stanley sat was low-backed and narrow in the seat. It was so low that Stanley's knees bumped up to throw his lap into a miniature ski slope. He solved the problem by keeping his feet stretched out in front of him in comfort. A glass and a bottle of Passport scotch whiskey rested on the end table beside him. Beside it was a bowl of ice cubes, a ready supply of which Judith kept available in the plastic trays she had brought with her from the States. Outside the country's expensive foreign tourist hotels, the availability of ice cubes locally was as rare as an appearance of the yeti.

Judith sat back in an easy chair beside her desk, in her weekend-casual jeans and dark blue mohair sweater looking like a somewhat plump, intelligent, not bad-looking graduate student. Her heavy tortoise shell eyeglasses compounded that appearance. Her seeming plumpness reflected the extra sweater and woolen undergarments that she, like everyone else in the north climate, donned increasingly as the weather turned colder. A sheaf of papers she was reading rested on a clipboard on her lap. Stanley had his own piles of student papers beside him on the sofa. The necessary task of reading and correcting batches of often similarly dull answers to questions seemed much less onerous in this pleasant atmosphere of shared experience.

Anyone observing the scene might have thought of the two of them as an old married couple comfortably whiling away a Friday night. For each of this couple, however, the easy but strong friendship and companionship served its own purpose of academic, social and, occasionally, personal reinforcement, as true friendships are apt to do. Stanley had come to feel as much at home in Judith's living room as he did in his own.

"Here. Listen to this." Stanley rattled a paper, laughing as he did so. He read,

"'The plot of the dream itself is unbelievable but true tragedy to normal people of all society. The new king of trait-u-ous gift,'" read Stanley, sounding out the written syllables ponderously, "'is a murth- - er-er.'" He repeated "murther-er-er" for emphasis, and then went on. "'Such a virtuous queen abandons the former king's celestial bed and states to the incestuous—'" He hesitated, trying to make out the handwritten script. "'The young fiancée, Ophelia, stands betraying on the side of Hamlet's uncle, who is his own stepfather.'"

Judith was shaking with laughter.

"Wait," Stanley raised a hand. "That's not all."

He continued to read,

"'The in-cread-able plot ends in the destruction of all instant people, and also dest-rous Hamlet, the revenger, who is a tragic character.'"

"Well, he got that right," Stanley interspersed. He went on, "'Fact-ing the hurrible murther of his father, he hesitates between 'to be or not to be.' Hamlet, as an idealist, de-cedes not to be, for he can't understand that some human beings would rather commit mur-thur for lust for crown, also his heart is torn to pieces so at finally he is sent to death by the author. The end.'"

"I should think so!" Judith laughed merrily.

"Seriously, though," Stanley placed the paper on the pile beside him, and slapped at it. "How can I work with this kind of student? This boy is in my third-year class. One of those papa-paying, affluent students. A college junior!"

"I wish I wrote Chinese that well," Judith responded amiably.

"Judith, you know what I mean."

"Of course I do. Just keep teaching him, Stanley. He'll be one hundred per cent better this time next year! They come a long way in a year, working with the rather insane foreign language of English."

Stanley puffed his cheeks and made an explosive sound in mock exasperation. "'You wish!' as the kids say."

They continued to read, each absorbed in his own work. Stanley suddenly exploded with laughter.

"Oh my God! listen to this. 'I have chosen the poem by the English Keats, about King Lear. He tells his wife, 'O Queen of far away! Leave melodizing on this wintry day. Shut up pages, and be mute. . .' Lear is asking his wife to shut up because he is thinking heavily about the eternal theme of life.'"

Judith grinned. She raised an eyebrow.

"You know, Stanley, that's a more sanguine interpretation of what Keats is writing about than many august scholars have come up with." She added, smiling, "except for the Muse being Lear's wife, of course."

For a time the only sound in the room was the scratching of pens against paper, or when one or the other of the two friends made a comment on a particularly notable theme.

After a quiet spell of reading, Stanley was aware of Judith, with a heavy sigh, saying,

"Stanley, excuse me."

Stanley looked up from a particularly diffuse paragraph, made more so by the aid of a very dangling participle.

"This is the paper I mentioned earlier that I'd like you to look at, Stanley. It's awfully good. Probably the best paper I have. And it should be. Li

Jian is the top student in the class. He's hoping to win one of the two scholarships to Mohegan this year. But something about it doesn't jibe. I can't place it, but I'd swear I've read at least some of the passages somewhere before." She swirled the blue binder with the fancy calligraphy across the space between them. He caught it in an outstretched hand.

He began to skim the pages of the paper, slowly at first, and then riffling through to the middle, where he read an entire page. He cut to the final paragraphs.

"My God!" he uttered. He sat up, planted both feet against the floor, then leaned over to pick up his drink and take a sip from the glass.

"What is it?" Judith rested a finger at the end of a line marking where she had stopped reading. But in the next second she was to lose her place completely. For Stanley was saying,

"Why, this is Wang Jun's paper. Wang Jun was a student of mine about three years ago. After she graduated, she was sent to Germany for graduate study. She wrote this here for my linguistics course, I think, when she was a junior." He had begun to leaf through the paper again. "Brilliant. Parts of it seem to have been cut out here and there-- but I'd know this paper anywhere!"

"Oh, shit!" escaped from Judith.

"Uh, uh." Stanley faked looking shocked at Judith's using the 'shit.' "Remember what you said to Woofy about teachers' use of the vernacular!"

Judith tried to laugh, but was obviously too distraught to do more than force a false smile.

"Oh, Stanley, what do I do? I had such high hopes for that young man! Do you know Li Jian?"

Stanley pursed his lips and shook a finger at Judith. He sat straight up on the couch, a stern expression on his face, which had gone red. "Don't go sentimental on me, Judith. I don't know the kid, but he's a cheater. If he were my student, I'd have him expelled." He frowned. "Teach the rest of them a lesson. They're all cheating now, since the reform. It's a kind of open market capitalistic philosophy with no Confucian ethic. Buy what you can, sell what you can, cheat where you can. Keep ahead of the other guy if you plan to succeed. If Lenin knew of such pragmatic goings on, he would, as they say, turn in his grave. You'll probably just have the boy's wrists slapped a little."

"Stanley, are you lecturing me?"

Stanley realized the index finger of his right hand was still pointed toward Judith. He quickly lowered his hand, laying it flat on the open binder in his lap and looked up at Judith with an amused smile on his face.

"Well, yes, I suppose so. I suppose I am. Sorry." He added, "Why, do you mind being lectured?"

"No, of course not." She smiled warmly at him.

"Why not? Occupational dis-ease." He grinned, and reached for his glass, which now he found empty. "May I fix myself a fresh drink? This subject demands it." Laying aside onto the couch the blue binder, he rose and headed for the kitchen to find some fresh ice cubes.

"Which subject is the occupational disease?" Judith called out. "Plagiarism or lecturing me?"

Over the rattle from her refrigerator as he dislodged the ice cube tray, she heard,

"Both. Why not?"

As he returned to the couch, Judith said,

"Would you like a sandwich or some sort of snack?"

"Mm-mm. A sandwich would be great."

Judith went off into the kitchen. After a few minutes, she returned with a plate of several small ham sandwiches, which she offered to Stanley. He took one off the top.

"Thank you."

She set the plate down on the cocktail table in front of him, picked up a sandwich for herself and went back to her desk. She hadn't realized how hungry she was and was glad she had remembered to pick up the half loaf of white bread from the canteen on her return to her apartment in the afternoon. Although Judith usually ate only lunch in the foreigners' dining room downstairs, she had made an arrangement with Lao Wang, the elder cook, to purchase daily from the kitchen a supply of the uniquely small-sized but delicious white bread he had learned to make so well for the foreigners. Lao Wang was said to have an "iron rice bowl," meaning he could never be removed from his job as chief cook without his consent. He was over seventy years old now, but still appeared in the kitchen every morning. Most of the daily cooking was left to the three younger men in the kitchen. But to the delight of the foreign teachers and students at Shi Da, Lao Wang continued faithfully to produce each day some delicious Western baked goods a Christian missionary to Shenshang had taught him how to make sixty years ago. Some days it was loaves of the small, white bread; at other times, it was muffins or Danish pastries. Judith especially loved the strawberry Danish.

Meanwhile, Stanley had lifted the fresh white bread from the top of his sandwich and was looking at what was inside.

"Where did you get this Sichuan ham?" He smacked his lips appreciatively.

"I bought a couple of tins in Beijing, when I was there in August."

Stanley chuckled and, looking up at the ceiling, recited with mock ponderousness,

"Foreign ways and foreign sins,
Fishy things in fishy tins,
All of these are very odd
And not at all the ways of God."

"That's wonderful!" Judith cried. "Where in the world did you get that?"

"Made it up from something I heard a missionary saying one day," grunted Stanley. "Anyway, how do you suppose they cure this ham differently from all the other smoked ham in the world? It is delicious! What makes it so special?"

Judith had not really thought much about it. "I suppose Sichuan farmers have a special diet for their pigs."

"Ha!" Stanley said, raising an index finger in the air. "I know. They feed the pigs that wonderful hot and sour soup!"

"As a first course!" They both broke into loud giggles.

Stanley said, "Remember those inner city kids from New York who went up to the country for a summer holiday? And when one little girl finally saw a live pig, she said, 'Oh, how gross! I'll never eat a pork chop again.' Judith, maybe it's better we don't know the culinary habits of the Sichuan pig!"

They returned to reading the student papers. The room was quiet for a while, until Judith said, "Oh, Stanley, I'm really so upset about this Li Jian business. What a mess!" She banged the desk. "Just what we don't need right now. I'll have to do something about it pretty quick."

"'You were right, dahlin'." He heard himself echoing one of Shelby's favorite expressions, 'Dahlin'! he pursued, "the correct word is *shit!*" He closed the folder he had been reading, and looked over at her. "At any rate, I'll get you the original from the files."

He began gathering up his paraphernalia. His watch read almost eleven o'clock. Late for a small northeast China university town. The *fuwuyuan* would have already locked the outside doors of the building. He placed the blue binder with the plagiarized manuscript on the ledge of Judith's couch to keep it separate from his own papers. After a few more minutes of conversation about the unfortunate turn of events in Li Jian's aspirations, he bade Judith a fond, if strictly verbal, goodnight, and climbed the stairs to his room.

Chapter 15
Karaoke

Not far from campus was a small restaurant, very popular on weekends. The *jiaozi*, dumplings, it served were deliciously seasoned, cooked to order, and well within student means. Local beer was plentiful and cheap, as was *bingqilin*, ice cream, for those who preferred that to the popular amber of northeast China. Especially during meal times, the tiny room was filled with students drinking and smoking, eating and socializing.

On most evenings between six thirty and nine thirty, in the bowels of the restaurant at the back of the alley, another room, large with booths partially curtained off and dark, was open to a select public. Two restaurant security men checked in through a back door on the outside those students and other eligible patrons who passed their undefined entrance requirements. Those not favored with admission were simply told that the karaoke bar was "closed." Any doubt in the minds of those being turned away was reinforced by one of the uniformed security guards casually patting his gun in its holster as he allowed the cigarette dangling from his mouth casually to drop to the ground, where he extinguished it with the heel of his boot.

Inside, in the dimly lighted cocktail bar, following the purchase of drinks, a patron could in his turn mount a stage at the front of the room, and sing, for whomever of the assembled audience cared to pay attention, any of a number of karaoke selections, the words to which appeared in Chinese, Japanese, or English, on a large screen. "I Left My Heart in San Francisco" was a particular favorite in all three languages. As the singer belted out, or whispered--some female singers were apt to be demure, if not shy,--the delights of that famed American city, both the singer and the audience vicariously looked over San Francisco from The Top of the Mark. They splashed into the stunning blue waves of the ocean, bounded in a bright red convertible over Russian Hill, rode a cable car, and, finally, held hands with a lover over a plate of prawns in a Fisherman's Wharf restaurant.

The treasures of the karaoke bar did not end here. The management maintained also a fine, if limited, reputation of being a place where businessmen or lovers were able to meet in the small booths curtained off from the public for personal trysts. The owners did not concern themselves with whether these private meetings were about foreign trade, local business, or were romantic encounters. Continued legitimacy for any of these supplementary facilities to the restaurant centered on discretion and the friendly relations existing between the restaurant owners and the local police.

Over the startling and unexpected screech of a tiny young woman slaving away at the English language in her version of "Love Is a Many-Splendored Thing" with the microphone a little too close to her face, Stanley was attempting to explain to Shelby the intricacies of the local entertainment operation.

"It's a Chinese-Japanese economic joint venture!" he shouted over the din. The two teachers were seated near the back of the room, where a ubiquitous loudspeaker covered their corner. The room was crowded on a Friday night for the popular karaoke, the innovative nostrum from Japan that had turned salary men into Frank Sinatras for the golden moment they held the microphone. Aspiring girl singers approached the stage to rival Madonna. This inventive entertainment, for those who could afford it, changed normally shy men and women into ego-driven maniacs. Watching a suited man in his forties who looked like a visiting Japanese business man from Tokyo or Kyoto emote "Stardust" in Japanese for the third time to the loud applause of his Chinese table companions, Shelby remembered what a coach of amateur dramatics had once remarked to her: "It's hard as hell to get them on the boards. It's IMPOSSIBLE to get them off!"

"How did you find out about this place?" She hoped she could be heard above the crackling microphone.

"A police officer I know downtown, a Chief Inspector Ling Feng, brought me here one evening." Stanley lifted the large bottle of beer the waiter had left on their table, and was topping off their glasses.

Shelby said, "You seem to have a lot of friends in different places." Professor Poussaint was turning out to be a more interesting man than she had first suspected.

"Oh, look, there's Elaine!" She tapped Poussaint on the arm as she suddenly spotted their colleague through the crowd in the throw-off light from the screen across the room. Shelby waved, but Elaine apparently could not see her through the smoke-filled dimness of the room.

Shelby could not see whom she was with. She peered more closely. It looked like Li Jian, her own student who was introducing her to so many of the good local restaurants, and who was so anxious to win the scholarship to Mohegan University.

Well, that was enterprising of Elaine! She hadn't mentioned any social acquaintance with the student.

Stanley was saying, "As long as these guys pay their taxes to the government way up front, and the necessary small handouts here and there, they can do very well in business now the wraps are off. But a lot of foreigners don't understand how Chinese business works, so they get frustrated and unhappy, and blame the Chinese." The music ended abruptly, and Stanley stopped in mid-sentence, looking around to ascertain whether his voice in the sudden quiet had attracted attention. No one seemed to be paying any special attention to Shelby and him. Some people had begun to leave. The table near theirs had ordered more bottles of beer, and its occupants were now toasting each other with raised glasses, calling out *Ganbei*!

"Bottoms up!" A Westerner and a Chinese in a partly closed off booth were having what appeared to be a serious business conversation.

Shelby said, "When I was on the way to Shen Shang, I met some Chinese suits in Hong Kong who were very upset about business methods here on the mainland."

"True enough. Some of the overseas Chinese in the West, or Hong Kong, lose sight of the traditional Mainland Chinese business methods, if they knew much about them in the first place."

The music started up again. Someone turned up the volume to ear blast.

"Do you think I can find the *cesuo*? Shelby suddenly had to pee badly. Beer did that to her.

"Ask the *fuwuyuan* at the bar!" Stanley yelled. She stood and walked in the direction of the bar, a little miffed that Stanley had not even noticed that she had learned the word for toilet in her Chinese lesson this week. He just seemed to take knowing Chinese phrases for granted. Just because *he* spoke supposedly good Mandarin didn't mean she or any of the other teachers did, too. Although Woofy, that young Chinese American Wu Fang, must surely know a lot of Chinese, too. She was a funny one, that one, with her blond young Schwarzenegger of a husband, Taylor. What a pain of post teenagers! Yuck! She shook her shoulders in a little shiver as she made her way around the bar, from there following her nose to a closet-sized cubicle with a hole-in-the-ground Turkish toilet you had to squat down over. She wished she could have waited until she got back to her dorm. At least the Foreign Guest Home had decent Western toilets.

On her return to the room from toilet facilities she preferred not to dwell on, she edged around the far side of the bar to say hello to Elaine and Li Jian. But another couple occupied the upholstered sofa where they had been sitting. There was no sign of them.

Chapter 16
A Modest Proposal

Early November

It was such a lovely day, sunny and windless. Judith wished she were enjoying it. But, since Zhang Jingchun's visit to her flat last evening, and their subsequent walk in the park with its disastrous results, she had been unable to put away a feeling of guilt and depression, depression because she wished the situation causing it could have been avoided, guilt because, well, because he seemed to have misinterpreted their friendship, as well as the truth of her feelings. She had spoken to no one about it, but all day both he and she had seemed either too embarrassed or angry to speak or look at the other directly. She felt it best to avoid him.

Zhang Jingchun and Judith Treadway, department chairman and as senior foreign expert, had known each other for almost seven years now. As colleagues and as friends, they got on extremely well despite, or perhaps because of, radically different backgrounds: she, a child of democracy, he, a product of Mao Zedong's socialist revolution, as well as of the devastating Cultural Revolution, and numerous social and political regimes. A kind, extremely considerate man, Zhang Jingchun had nevertheless proved himself a strong, able administrator. He was a political survivor. In academic matters, he and Judith shared the discharge of a common philosophy and purpose, both in teaching and in relations with the department.

There were, of course, considerable matters involving the administration of the English Department of a reputable Chinese university with a staff of over a dozen local teachers, with whom the foreign experts and teachers had little to do. Professor Judith Treadway's own area involved mainly the direction and teaching of the department's sections on "American Literature," as everyone insisted on calling it, despite her efforts to have it referred to as U.S. literature, out of deference to the significant numbers of important Canadian, Mexican and Latin American writers, living and dead, who were also American writers. However, one can't win 'em all, Judith told herself, feeling it prudent not to beat this particular drum too hard.

She enjoyed her courses in contemporary drama and poetry, as well as administering the scholarship and student exchange programs between the sister universities of Mohegan in the U.S. and Shi Tong University here in China. That program was now in its fifth year of successful operation, despite political and economic changes and the usual bureaucratic hassles. Judith gratefully gave Zhang Jingchun full credit for the success of the joint-venture academic program.

Prior to last evening, there had never been a notion of personal attachment between the two of them other than a fine camaraderie in their common work and the recreational activities and dinners they more often than not shared with the community, as they did the Friday Night Club activities, for example. She harbored no romantic notions about him. How astonishing, then, that last night he had appeared at her flat at about eight o'clock, proposing she go for a stroll over campus with him. It being a mild, pleasant night, she had agreed. There was a full moon, and a light snow was falling.

When they reached the little park across the quadrangle, he had taken a handkerchief from his pocket and, brushing some snowflakes from a park bench, he had placed the square of cloth on the bench, motioning for her to sit. He stood close to her at the end of the bench, silent, as, companionably, she thought, they had looked up appreciatively—though to her mind, not romantically—at the white moon and the star-filled sky. Finally, he broke the stillness.

"May I ask you a question?" His breathing was uneven. Judith could sense a feeling of nervous hesitation in his usually confident tone of voice. She looked up at his kind face, which she could see quite clearly in the moonlight.

"He said, "I need someone to work with me forever."

She nodded, and smiled up at him. A few silver snowflakes fell against his cheek.

He cleared his throat, and continued, "I need a person to cook for me forever." He paused, "to take care of me forever." Suddenly he was touching her shoulder, then caressing her hair. "Someone to live with me forever." His words were a whisper. "Judith, do you think you may be the right person to do that?"

Her shock was so great that she had leapt up from the bench before she realized what she was doing, leaving his hand in midair as she stumbled away from his grasp. Almost immediately, she turned back toward him, embarrassed at the childishness of her reaction. But it was too late; the harm had been done. He had straightened his shoulders and straightened his hat on his head, turning abruptly away from her as he did so.
No more had been said.

At the doorway of the Foreigner's Guest House, he held the door open for her. "I'm sorry for my outburst," he said, his expression frozen as he looked straight at her. "Good night to you."

She could feel the oppressive distance between them like a wall. She had never felt so rebuked and far away from him, as though she had treated him like a stranger who had unexpectedly winked at her in the subway, making her turn and scurry away. She knew enough of Chinese manners to know what the recent effort had cost him, the consideration and importance attached to such a proposal—especially to a foreigner—not lightly made. Things could never be the same between them again. How she wished she could have spared him the loss of face her rejection cost him. He must have hoped for the triumph of reason and even romance. Under the affable exterior, he was not a man whose decisions were made lightly. She had an odd feeling he would not forgive her this singular rebuke to his pride.

Chapter 17
Zhang Jingchun Reflects

Zhang Jingchun sat at his desk, reviewing the day's stack of letters, notices, leaders' administrative directives for his ongoing duty. A new group of Russian tourists was scheduled to arrive on the noon plane from Beijing tomorrow. Yu Hong, the office administrative assistant, had already been ordered to arrange the mini-bus to meet them. The customary welcome dinner was scheduled for five o'clock, he noted. He must attend; it was part of his official duties.

Riffling through the pile of correspondence on his desk, he picked up a handwritten note from one of the foreign teachers: Teacher Johnson was distressed that her salary had not been paid on time. He'd have to telephone the Foreign Affairs Office and talk politely with his friend, the deputy administrator, to try to arrange to have the foreigners' salary paid on the regular due dates. Several foreign teachers had complained about not being paid on the days officially designated as "salary payment days," especially during holiday periods. Patience was not a western virtue, especially when it came to money.

The department's weekly meeting for Chinese faculty and staff was scheduled for four o'clock in the afternoon, as usual. Of course he was expected to attend. He was hungry, but reminded himself that he would have a good dinner when he finally got home at six o'clock. His sister had promised to prepare food for him today. Meanwhile, he should read again the schedule of the Russian experts who were arriving with the tour group. Under the new joint-venture program, he would be permitted to go to Russia in two months' time, to arrange for additional student exchanges. It would be good to travel, even into Russia with its continuing economic difficulties that often weighed upon the student exchanges. What was most important was keeping up the flow of students between the two countries.

Under the current policy, the university tried to maintain good relations with all countries now, both East and West. He would do his duty. Good comrades did their duty. The interpreter Sun Jing was assigned to accompany him on this trip, he noted, reading the notice. She was the most experienced Russian-Chinese translator in the joint foreign language departments, he thought, and certainly the most conscientious, although a few foreign experts had on occasion complained about her great interest in their private possessions, about which he had had to admonish her. When she went to their rooms to explain a program to them, she seemed always to find in their rooms some items of interest that she wanted to know about: books, food, tapes on their tape machines. One of the Russian experts had actually accused her of being a Chinese spy. The Chairman had of course reassured him that she was just a curious young woman, who wanted to know about other countries' customs. The Russian expert was not convinced, but he was polite.

Here in China, in the old days, all of the Soviet comrades had been individualistic about possessions, proud of their watches and Chinese leather jackets they bartered for on the free market with their own fur hats and coats. They were enterprising in trading everything of value they could bring with them to China. But they were distrusting of the Chinese, who regarded them as Westerners and foreigners as much as they, of course, regarded their hosts, the Chinese, as Asian foreigners, not to be trusted. Diplomacy with all foreigners was delicate. There were other problems with which he had to deal, with the Foreign Affairs Office regarding the Americans. Teacher Shelby Johnson had not shown up for class today. He had telephoned her flat.

"No, I did not go to class today. I just could not take any more!" she said, after six rings had brought her to the telephone. "I will not put up with the Waiban refusing to pay my extra baggage allowance...It was bad enough that my luggage arrived here three months late! And then, Mr. Power (the foreigners' sly, joking name for Yang Youli) said to me that, as a good friend of China, I should know better than to complain!

The Chairman made several telephone calls, at the same time as he cleared his desk. Finally, he permitted himself to stop and think for a moment about what had depressed and discouraged him all day.

He had waited for such a long time of his life before ever thinking of marrying again. So much of his memory was devoted to his dead wife, a wonderful woman, so sweet and loving. Although their marriage had been an arranged one, love had sprung up quickly between the two young people, and nurtured by care and thoughtfulness, had grown into the strongest feelings of his lifetime. Then had come the tragedy. She, whose delicacy had not withstood those bitter, cold winters of deprivation during the Cultural Revolution in the 1970's, had simply and suddenly died of blood poisoning. Two years before her untimely death, he had publicly denounced himself and burned his lyrical poems, agreeing with the Political Committee that his simple poems about nature were reactionary, and the product of bourgeois capitalistic thinking. He had agreed to anything just to have private peace, away from the public criticism of his writing from the local Citizen Committee. But his wife had not recovered from having to kneel on shards of glass because a neighbor had "accused" her, having one day overheard her singing an American western song, "Red River Valley." His wife loved that song, and sang it beautifully, imitating a phonograph record his own mother had owned when they lived in Shanghai when he was a child. It took all his strength not to cry when he heard that song being played so freely these days over the public loudspeakers.

It had taken him a long time, too, to convince himself that the old life was past, and that the new China, his motherland which he loved dearly, would not allow him a fresh opportunity for a happy life.

He was thinking now how the American professor Judith Treadway, a compassionate person so sympathetic to Chinese traditions and culture, had for the past year seemed to him an ideal solution to the quest for companionship and affection in this latter part of his life. She had appeared to him to be perhaps even good fortune, a happy fortune. He did not like at all the heavy feeling of disappointment that was overcoming him when he reflected on her abrupt behavior to him last evening. No one had a right to treat him in this fashion again, after what he had suffered.

Although never articulate about his personal emotions, he had finally decided to speak to her, to propose marriage. Her rejection had humiliated him.

Sometime later, still seated at his desk, he jolted himself back to the reality of his office, aware that his mind was besotted with more than unkind thoughts, thoughts unworthy of his own mastery of self, certainly. He felt himself possessed by the very devil of anger and abasement.

He attempted to clear his head. He was tired and hungry; he wanted to go home. While he stood and looked out of the window below, the back door to the outside compound squeaked. As he watched, he saw Judith Treadway cross the courtyard. In her green

People's Army greatcoat, which she had bought in the free market earlier in the year, when they had been walking out together, she moved across the quadrangle, her head and shoulders wrapped in the oversized white knitted scarf she favored in the cold weather. She huddled into the wind as she hurried to get out of its brutal path and off into the Foreign Guest House, he reasoned. It had begun to snow, just a few moments ago. Now it fell heavily, large flakes mastering the wind to swirl to the ground, which had already become white.

As Judith crossed over the ground's surface, footprints broke the lightly snowed cement courtyard into two unequal quadrilaterals, like the illustration for a problem in geometrical measurement.

Dr. Zhang continued to look out of the window, watching the wind and snowflakes obliterate her footprints, leaving the courtyard without a trace of anyone's having crossed it. As abruptly as it had begun, the snow stopped, leaving a flat white surface.

Chapter 18
Wu Fang Provides a Solution

Her watch said a quarter to three. She had made the appointment for three o'clock at the small coffee shop, which she knew would be uncrowded, as most of the students had classes at that hour. Wu Fang gathered together the papers she had been trying to correct, and stuffed them into the tan leather, professional-looking briefcase Taylor had given her for a wedding present. She picked up the envelope that lay in front of her on the desk, and, for the third time that hour, carefully counted the Chinese yuan in it. She placed the envelope in the briefcase, which she snapped shut. She pulled tight the door of the office she shared with three Chinese teachers in the English department and moved down the hall to the front stairs and exited the building. The coffee shop was just across the east campus, not five minutes away.

The décor of the coffee shop was an arranged marriage between art deco and low camp. The entire room was lighted from a single pink and green plastic fixture attached to the mirrored wall at the service area. The non-functioning chandelier hanging from the ceiling gave the room a decadent look, along with the dust it reflected. The walls were a dark chocolate. Multicolored tinsel chains dangled at whimsy from ceiling and wall. The balloon coming out of the mouth of a laughing Donald Duck painted on the window at the entrance signaled that steamed dumplings were available on request.

Xiao Mei, the young woman student Wu Fang had arranged to meet, was waiting in a booth toward the back of the room. She looked small and scared, nodding her head in acknowledgement of the other's entrance. Wu Fang strode to the back booth, without speaking, smiling a calculated smile geared to ease the other woman's defenses. Neither woman removed her coat, although the room was not cold.

"I'll have a coffee," Wu Fang said to the *fuwuyuan* who appeared at the table in a dirty white apron, then stood, staring at the wall. The waitress appeared to have no interest in her two customers other than to listen to their orders. After denying twice Wu Fang's offer of drink or food, Xiao Mei whispered that, yes, she would like a *chaobing*, the bland sherbet popular among students year round, weather notwithstanding. The waitress yelled the order over to a middle-aged woman at the service counter, then retreated in the direction of the kitchen. A minute later, she reappeared, holding the ice cream bar in her hand. Picking up Wu Fang's coffee order from the counter, she carried it to the booth and slid it onto the table, the coffee sloshing into the saucer and onto the tabletop. She plopped the ice cream in front of Xiao Mei, and disappeared back into the kitchen.

"You are very kind to talk to me." Xiao Mei had lowered her eyes as she began to speak. Her next words were unintelligible. Wu Fang leaned forward to hear her clearly. The pregnant bitch was very confused and easily intimidated; she felt that at once. The timid worm also had an annoying nervous habit of pulling at strands of her long black hair, then examining the hair carefully while avoiding looking at Wu Fang. Wu Fang tried to control her impulse to slap the hair out of the woman's hand as a means to get her complete attention. She was repeating in Chinese and English each sentence she said to Xiao Mei.

"You understand completely what I am teaching you," she said, then translated her words into Mandarin Chinese. Her stern gaze bore into the younger woman's face. "No harm will some to you if you do exactly as I have told you to do."

Xiao Mei was nodding in agreement, her hair falling over her face. With a hand, she pushed strands of it back out of the way. There were tears in her eyes.

Wu Fang removed the envelope from her briefcase, and placed it on the table.

"It is settled, then." Her gaze bore relentlessly into Xiao Mei. "You will leave immediately for your village."

The plan was perfect, Wu Fang thought to herself. The envelope held enough money for the trip and the abortion, as well as a tidy sum that would feed and otherwise take care of Xiao Mei for some time, as well as making possible the purchase of gifts for the grandmother with whom she would be staying. The bitch understood that she was not to see Taylor ever again. His career was too important for it to be ruined by vile gossip and scandal. Being a decent girl, Wu Fang stressed, Xiao Mei would disappear, and take all necessary steps to erase the unfortunate incident from their lives.

Reaching into her bag, Wu Fang placed in front of Xiao Mei a packet of paper tissues to stem the tears and runny nose of the younger woman, whose face was now a blotch of mottled red. Seemingly not seeing the tissues on the table, Xiao Mei took from her coat pocket a crumpled piece of letter paper, into which she loudly and fully blew her nose.

Wu Fang reached across the table to touch the girl on the shoulder, as though to solace her. At the same time, she said, "What is most important is that you do not return to this town, no way! Ever, nor communicate with anyone!" She emphasized her words with a grip on the shoulder which, while appearing to offer comfort, at the same time displayed a pressure that signaled a special message of power. With a whimper, Xiao Mei lowered her head to the table. Wu Fang withdrew her hand. The envelope still lay on the table between them. Xiao Mei blew her nose again. Then she said, in a hardly audible mumble,

"Professor Treadway says, that after some-time—"

Wu Fang froze.

"Professor Treadway? What does she have to do with it?"

"*Laoshi* says if I must leave the school for personal, it is important that I return and work and graduate." She sniffed. "She is kind to my situation of leaving now."

"You must not come back!" Wu Fang was close to shouting. "Not while my husband and I are here. Do you understand that?" She lowered her voice. It was exacting and harsh. At the same time, she took from her purse and slammed onto the table at Xiao Mei's side a tube of Chinese brand lipstick labeled "Tao Hua Kou Hong."

"Here's your Peach Flower Red Mouth," she hissed. "It was in my husband's raincoat pocket." The lipstick tube rolled off the table into Xiao Mei's lap. A look of guilt suffused the girl's face.

Xiao Mei began to sob, uttering small soprano cries of pain. Wu Fang reached over and grasped her again by the shoulder, this time so hard that Xiao Mei was forced to look Wu Fang full in the face.

"You are hurting me!" she whimpered. Her face betrayed her desperation, even as she tried not to move her body, but to hold herself stiff against her adversary.

"Terrible things will happen to you if you even think of returning!" Wu Fang emitted an ugly curse. The girl found herself trembling against her will.

The expression of hatred on Wu Fang's face was dreadful. With one hand still clutching the unfortunate shoulder, she held her eyes on Xiao Mei, as, with her other hand, she pushed the envelope forward like a juggernaut. It fell into the younger woman's lap. Wu Fang watched as Xiao Mei slowly folded it in thirds, so that it fit into the small shoulder strap purse by her side.

Only then did Wu Fang release her hold on the girl. The two of them sat for a moment in silence.

Then, in the manner of a hostess bidding farewell to her guests after a successful party, Wu Fang extended her hands palms upward.

"You see, it's not so difficult, after all. Everything will be just fine." She added, "In your own future life. *Taihaola!* Just fine!"

Chapter 19
Stanley Goes for a Swim

Lanes three through ten of the Olympic-size pool were lined with splashing young men racing against each other like a company of highly disciplined water bugs. The boys appeared to be between the ages of eight and eighteen. They were the brightest and the best of the province's young athletes. Having proved themselves at the local level, through hard work combined occasionally with political favoritism, these strong, healthy, young athletes were currently being groomed to compete in China's sports at the national level and, with growth and determination, in a coming year's ASIAD or even full Olympics.

As each swimmer reached the end of his lane, a coach reached down a hand to haul him up out of the pool. Immediately the coach would go into a huddle with the young swimmer, sometimes demonstrating a particular arm or leg motion, sometimes just bending over to confer, arm around his charge's shoulder in an uncle-like fashion, to explain a particular point of importance which the swimmer acknowledged by nodding his head as he bent to shake water out of an ear. With a slight push or a slap on the behind, the coach would send the lad hurtling back into the water to practice his corrected race stroke.

In swim trunks and with a towel slung over his shoulder, Stanley entered the pool area and walked to the diving end of lanes one and two, the section reserved for cadres and other important visitors. He shivered slightly as he walked the length of the pool. The room was not warm, although for China the pool was a very heated one. He felt lucky to have a pass to this very private and exceedingly well-equipped sports complex, normally unknown to the foreigners. As usual, he silently thanked his friend Police Chief Inspector Ling Feng, who had been of considerable help in making Stanley feel at home in China, as well as welcome in many areas of recreation, the existence of which was neither visible nor imagined by ordinary people, Chinese or foreign.

As a result of their liaison over the past several years, Stanley enjoyed several distinct advantages over his proletarian foreign colleagues, as well as the mass of the Chinese public, most of whom would never have a notion this pool with its accoutrements existed. At least twice a week, Stanley managed a swim and a one-to-three-mile walk on the excellent and expensive foreign Stridator in the exercise room. He also lifted weights and rowed on the rowing machine when the spirit – or the body – moved him.

Now he settled down to his usual fifty laps. He tightened the strap of his dark underwater glasses and attached the nosepiece, then dove into the first of the two lanes cordoned off from the young swimmers' training area.

He had completed about twelve laps when the arm of a swimmer in the next lane bumped him, putting him off stride. An old cadre poking up and down the water, he thought. He raised his head briefly to look over the water. Whoever had wandered into his lane had gone ahead in the other direction. He bent back into the water and continued pacing himself, completing each lap smoothly and uniformly without pause.

When he completed his stint to satisfaction, he swam to the edge of the pool and climbed out, flexing his legs on the stainless steel ladder.

He reached for his towel from the bench where he had left it. As he dried himself, he looked over the pool.

A tall young man in black string bathing trunks was approaching him, smiling. Stanley shook the water from his ears and his legs, and continued to towel himself.

"Professor Poussaint, what an excellent swimmer you are!"

"Hello, there," said Stanley, mustering cordiality to a stranger.

The young man stretched out a hand. "I was watching you."

Stanley raised his eyebrows in question.

"Can't a cat look at a king?" The Chinese boy grinned, displaying perfect white teeth. "Professor Treadway teaches us this little proverb."

Stanley swallowed to refrain from correcting the student's calling the line a proverb. Don't be a pompous ass, he told himself. Instead he asked, "You're from Shi Da?"

"Oh, yes, Professor."

Stanley's antenna picked up the young man's use of the "professor" in English, rather than the customary *Laoshi*. But this young man was not a student of his.

"What is your name?"

"Li Jian, Professor. I am a senior in Professor Treadway's class."

"Oh, yes, of course." As the youth spoke his name, Stanley's mind cut to the research paper Judith had showed him a few nights ago. So this was Li Jian, the student who, above or beyond honesty, would seem to have bought, or stolen, the Korzibski thesis of Stanley's former student.

"I am very sorry I intruded on your lane when you were swimming," the student was saying. "That is most discourteous. I apologize."

Stanley raised his hands, palms toward Li Jian, in protest. He was more interested in the lad's relaxed, man-to-man behavior, as though, despite the difference in age and station, they were two members of the same club who just happened to find themselves casually conversing. Which, in effect, they were.

"What brings you here, Professor?" Li Jian was saying.

"I might ask the same of you," Stanley returned. This was one smooth young man.

"Oh, my cousin is swimming coach here. So we, my brother and I, can come here anytime we like." He leaned back on one heel, arms folded in front of his chest, and looked proprietarily around the room.

Stanley agreed that the facilities were great. Li Jian said, with a small bow,

"I'm surprised, Professor, that I have not seen you here before. I have been swimming here several times since my cousin began the springtime training for the athletes."

Stanley chose to forego the efforts at familiarity. He merely nodded, as he continued to shuffle a small towel over his shoulders and back.

"Professor, when you are finished swimming, if you are otherwise not occupied, why don't you come with my cousin and me to have dinner, and drink some beer? We are going to a very fine restaurant not too far from here. My cousin has a car. We will be honored if you will join us."

"You are very kind, but I'm afraid I can't."

The boy appeared not to hear the refusal in Stanley's voice.

"Please, come and meet my cousin."

Letting Chinese politeness as well as his own curiosity about the scene win over his reluctance to continue conversation with the student, he walked the length of the pool with him, and over to where the man Stanley had earlier watched as he coached the young athletes busied himself hanging some flippers on nails ranged along the wall. The coach wore sweats. His hair was combed back neatly. He looked every inch the healthy, clean-living athlete.

"*Zhe shi wode laoshi*, this is my teacher," the student said to the coach.

Stanley shook hands with the man, who replied "Good Ev-en-ing" in courteously cautious English. He stood for a few seconds nodding his head and smiling at Stanley before he turned away to continue hanging up sets of flippers in orderly rows against the wall. Li Jian moved closer to the older man to speak directly at him.

Stanley gave no sign that he understood the conversation in Chinese between Li Jian and his cousin as the student spoke in low tones, trying to convince the older man to take them all out to a restaurant for dinner and drinks. It was evidently their first mention of dining out that evening. The coach pointed out the lateness of the hour. He also pointed out that "*tangxiongdi*," his "little cousin," was due back at the university in less than an hour. Li Jian appealed to the older man to help him "*Qing wode zhongyaode laoshi*," "invite my important teacher.". . . Stanley thought he detected a growing stutter in the aggressive young man's voice as he tried nervously to prevail over his cousin's remonstrations.

After a few moments, Stanley said, in English, "Li Jian, I must be getting back to the university. Please tell your cousin I have noticed him here before, and am very glad to meet him. He teaches the young swimmers very well."

With a final handshake to each of them, he left their company. He would have to tell Judith about this meeting. She'd be amused at the social shenanigans of young Li Jian, who either had a criminal mind or was stupid. In any event, he managed to convey the impression that the world existed largely to help him achieve his desired objectives, in one way or another.

Chapter 20
Elaine Discloses

In the kitchen, Shelby made herself a glass of Mango Tang, her favorite drink. Here in China, that was. She couldn't recall ever having tasted Mango Tang at home in the States; it must be a Chinese invention. The fruity-tasting drink had an exotic flavor, tart for a Chinese drink, but still very sugary; it satisfied her Louisiana sweet tooth. The batch tasted sweeter than usual. She went back into the kitchen, opened her little refrigerator and removed the miniscule ice cube tray. After holding it under the tap at the sink for almost a minute, she managed to extract some half-inch squares of ice. Good! She plopped them into her drink with pleasure.

She loved her kitchen. It was miniscule, too, just like her doll-size ice cubes, but just right for one person. And, of course, luxurious by Chinese standards. A two-burner gas range stood on a stainless steel counter unit. The built-in cabinet space under the counter held the staple ingredients of cooking oil, vinegar, and bottled sauces, as well as cleaning materials. A separate cupboard housed the propane gas tank that fed the burners. The entire space under the stove was enclosed in a tasteful charcoal-grey-painted wooden, three-door casing. Directly above the stove, a stainless steel vent supplied an exhaust fan and a fluorescent tube light which illuminated the stove wall. Laid out along the wall next to the vent, a series of small cabinets, also protected from dust and grease by the charcoal-colored formica doors, proved more than ample to hold Shelby's small stash of supplies from her shopping trip up to Beijing a few weeks ago.

She kept her secret supply of "CARE" goods from home—tuna fish, anchovies, lime and raspberry jello, which she adored—in a separate closet in her bedroom, not wanting to appear to show off to the other foreign teachers that she was the recipient of such goodies. Nor did she particularly wish to share them, except occasionally with Elaine, when they had their private "girls' night." Even then, she was a little wary of what she brought out on these occasions. Since Elaine refused to eat most Chinese food, she was more than apt to want to pig out on Shelby's delicacies. Last week, she had gobbled a whole jar of precious peanut butter.

A shoulder-high refrigerator and freezer combination, and a small, but deep local tiled sink completed the inventory of the furniture in her doll house kitchen. When Shelby first arrived, the refrigerator had occupied a prominent position in the living room. Despite the sign on the Foreign Teachers' bulletin board in the foyer downstairs, which stated that "Any Indoor Property May Not Be Moved Absolutely," she had one Sunday afternoon enlisted the aid of two students to have that refrigerator, which the Foreign Office considered a showpiece, moved out of the living room and into the tiny kitchen, where it just fitted in the small space behind the door. This meant that the kitchen door could never be entirely opened, so that no more than one person could conveniently occupy space in the tight little room at one time. That suited Shelby just fine. Her kitchen was her private treasure. She was stared at enough in the streets, and on campus. She had no wish to have visitors to her apartment poke around in her kitchen.

The Chinese were great at poking around. Most Chinese students or other visitors, on entering her flat, thought nothing of walking directly into her bedroom to look around, examine the furniture, comment on visible decorativeness, and openly inspect at some length any book or letter that happened to be lying on the desk. Such behavior seemed to be regarded as quite normal.

She had on occasion inquired from close Chinese acquaintances the reasoning behind what she, with her instilled background of the sacredness of privacy and property, considered curious conduct. She had been told that the Chinese concept of sharing common property overrode any notions of privacy. She wasn't sure how much she believed that. Her friendly informant had gone on to say, "Besides, we're very curious about foreigners," which seemed to her more likely the case.

At the knock on her door, she called out "*Jin lai!*" In the high-pitched voice she thought a good imitation of Chinese tonality.

"Why can't you just say, 'Come in'?" Elaine was pulling off her jacket as she hurried in against the cold draft in the hallway. "That southern accent just kills me! Jeee-in ly-eee!" She sank down on the couch in a burst of laughter, at the same time pulling to untie the laces of her Nike running shoes with both hands and pulling the sneakers off her feet. She wriggled her toes, then stretched her blue jean-encased long legs.

"You don't mind my un-laxing?"

"Make yourself at home, Daisy Mae." Shelby extended a hand graciously toward Elaine and made a short bow. She considered herself the perfect southern hostess.

"You surely knock me out, gal! But. . .Ah do have somethin' to tell you-all." Mindful of what she was about to impart, she straightened her back and then threw back her shoulders. She splayed her legs, digging her heels into the carpeting. The total effect was of a mechanical doll that had just run out of springs in the middle of its routine motions.

"Want some Mango Tang?" Shelby had disappeared into the kitchen. "I'm makin' some."

Yes, Elaine would have some. "But just with boiled water from the thermos. I don't trust your ice in that refrigerator." She picked up a copy of *Redbook* magazine from the coffee table, leafing through it with sharp, quick movements. Shelby saw she was jiggling her left foot, as though the spring to its mechanism was being wound up again.

"What's the matter, you nervous or something?" She giggled. "Or, maybe you have to go to the bathroom?"

"Matter of fact, yes. I mean, yes, I have to go to the bathroom. But that's not why I was jiggling my foot." She disappeared around the corner and out of the living room. The bathroom door banged closed.

Shelby set the cool drinks down on the little table, and settled herself in the chair opposite where Elaine had been sitting, to await her return.

She heard the toilet flush, and a moment later Elaine strode back into the room, and plopped herself again onto the couch. She snorted, "Well, your contraption back there seems to work! I'm afraid to use my john. That overhead pipe is still dripping. I'm afraid the damn ceiling will collapse on me again!" Two weeks ago, Elaine had regaled Shelby with the story of how she had entered her bathroom one morning to find that half the ceiling of the bathroom of her apartment had fallen on the floor during the night. "Thank the Almighty I wasn't in there!" Although she wouldn't have been really injured if she had been, "only scared shitless!" It turned out the ceilings in all the bathrooms of the Foreign Experts Building excepting the top floor were just sheets of decorative styrofoam, that were beginning to buckle and collapse whenever the toilet in the apartment overhead was flushed or otherwise leaked.

"Imagine! All this lover-ly socialist elegance," she said, as she swung her left arm in a wide arc about the room. "Millions of chandeliers, but no plumbing! My God!" She picked up her drink of Mango Tang with her free hand. "To the revolution!" Then, reminded of something else, she suddenly set her drink back down onto the glass table, and began to laugh until her entire body shook.

"I'm sorry, I just can't help it! Who said, 'The Chinese invented the wheel, but it turned out to be a Frankenstein'?" She was completely engrossed in her own mirth. She slapped her lap with her hands, and rocked back and forth.

"Oh, I forgot to tell you," she wagged a finger at Shelby, "and this is a serious business. I now keep an umbrella right beside the john, and hold it over my head whenever I need to go potty." She threw back her head and chortled, then in a quick gesture picked up the copy of *Redbook* from the table and began riffling through it again.

Shelby watched her for a minute, then, "So," she intoned, sipping at her drink, "What is so exciting in this beleaguered outpost of civilization that you ran here to tell me?"

Elaine dropped the magazine to the floor. "Oh! I got so distracted by that toilet I almost forgot!" She paused, and then went on. "Hah! This is not news for those innocent ones who want absolute certainty in an imperfect world. You are aware, my dear Shelby, of how Madame Judith handles this whole scholarship thing with Mohegan that she's in charge of? No level playing field, that!" She slapped at her lap, as if to punish it for Professor Treadway's attitude.

Shelby was well aware of the senior foreign expert's handling of the student exchange program, those scholarships so highly sought by senior students at Shi Tong. The scholarships, always highly prized since their inception, had now become especially precious because of a recent diplomatic moratorium on all but a few fortunate students being permitted to go abroad. But students from Shi Da who might be chosen under this program were said to be exempt from the current prohibition, as the long standing joint contract between the two universities had been signed long prior to any current regulations, and had another three years to run before completion of its terms.

"Well, Judith went into the Chair this morning, and advised Dr. Zhang that she is not accepting Li Jian's application for the U.S. scholarship to Mohegan. What's worse, she told him, she's not even considering it! She gives no reason. How's that for news?" Elaine grinned slyly.

"How can she do that? Li Jian is the Department's top student!" Shelby's eyes became enormous with surprise and disbelief. As his teacher, she was well aware that in addition to being nominated for a scholarship to Mohegan, he had won prizes in every local competition, as well as having ranked first in the competitive exams. Still, she reflected disconsolately, Judith, as Mohegan's senior representative in China, had free reign to act as she felt justified.

Apparently Elaine read her thoughts. She hissed, "Judith can do as she damn well pleases, and fucking does!" She leaned forward and imparted in a whisper, "Li Jian's fit to be tied!"

Shelby found herself wondering how Li Jian had come to learn so quickly the news of what had happened only this morning; and how Elaine knew quite so soon that he knew.

But Elaine was burbling on. "Do you know what else?" The energy being drained out of her by her outpourings caused her to stop in mid-sentence to plump herself back against the sofa, and put her feet up in a more comfortable position on the glass table.

Shelby waited patiently. One never could be certain what Elaine would come up with next. She always seemed to have the monopoly on all the latest local news.

"Well, it seems Madame Scholarship Chairman is going to make a new nomination. And do you know who?" Elaine exploded her cheeks. "Bhang Taur, that's who!"

Shelby looked puzzled. Bhong Taur was not a name she recognized from among her own students. She taught primarily students from the junior class.

Anyone being nominated for the Mohegan scholarship would have to be a senior. This being her own first year of teaching here, she wouldn't know any of last year's juniors, except for perhaps one or two of the new seniors who had been part of the official greeters when the foreign teachers had arrived on campus in late August. There had not been a Bhong Taur among them that she recalled.

"Bhong Taur?" she repeated. "Obviously one of her own students—"

"Oh, you know him. He's the kid from the mountains that rich American millionaire gave a library to—not Bhong Taur personally, but gave it to his village, that is." She added, "He's supposed to be pretty smart. But he usually stays to himself. You know, the kind that sits in the classroom at night and studies until hell turns into vanilla ice cream.

"But you and your bleeding heart—!" Elaine expostulated. She was bent over, grunting as she laced up her sneakers. "The ancestors will get you if you don't watch out! Listen, I gotta go." She struggled up out of the sofa.

"Zhang Jingchun must have had a heart attack."

"You can never tell about him." Elaine looked thoughtful. "When there are glitches in academe, he can be grumpy; but he's never churlish. I think he was pretty miffed. He announced the news at senior staff meeting this morning, which you missed. But he's such a sweet old goat - - he acted pretty calm. Besides, he's been through so much himself. I don't suppose a little thing like a student scholarship crisis could upset him one way or the other. If it did, you would never know it. He's a cool cat, man. Listen, I really gotta go."

And Elaine was out the door.

Chapter 21
A Midnight Caller

In what seemed the middle of the night, Stanley awakened abruptly. Opening one eye as little as he possibly could to enable him to read the fluorescent hands of the watch on his wrist against the pillow, he saw that it was five minutes past one o'clock. "A.M.," he muttered sleepily. Sixty-five minutes past midnight. He had just begun to doze off again when he heard the soft rapping at the outside door. He certainly was not expecting anyone at this hour.

Slipping a robe over his pajamas, he crossed into the living room. As he approached the outer door, he heard the sound again, a light repeated tapping, like a code. This time he recognized clearly that it was not his own door that was being rapped at. It was Elaine's, just down the corridor from him. He heard her latch click as it was slipped back. He managed to slide his own door open just in time to see the figure of a student he thought he recognized disappear through the doorway into her flat.

But how could any student have gotten into the locked building at this hour? The night reception *fuwuyuan* would not dare to let a local Chinese into the Foreign Guest House this late.

The student must have come into the building much earlier in the evening, somehow managing to circumvent the reception clerk so that he would not have signed the visitors' book as was required of all local visitors on entering and leaving. He could have hidden in the darkened ballroom or in the dining hall. It was a little frightening to contemplate that anyone who strongly wanted to do so could in fact easily slip by the reception desk if he was clever enough to do so; the *fuwuyuan* frequently sat behind the high counter, mostly hidden from view as they smoked and joked among themselves, so that a person caught their attention only with difficulty. The system of surveillance was only occasionally efficient; for most of the time, the officials relied on the students' and citizens' obedience to the strict rules, or fear of punishment, to enforce the prohibitions against unauthorized entry.

Stanley considered the risk of asking Elaine in the morning about her night visitor. He could not get back to sleep. He shifted uncomfortably and unsuccessfully from his right side to his left, punched his pillow to fluff it, and made several other fruitless attempts to comfort himself into sleep. He hoped this was not going to be another white night. He'd had several of those recently, and they left him tired and cranky in the mornings.

As he tried to drift into sleep, he found his mind turning on some of the occurrences and ideas that perplexed and vexed him these days in this new Changing China in which he had lived for the past several years. Although he was considered an "old

China hand," he found himself not infrequently confused by the lies and rumors that surrounded relationships between the Chinese teachers and the foreign teachers, for example, particularly where it related to exchange scholarships. Both teachers and students more than infrequently now falsified tests and achievements, making unbelievable assertions about their pasts (although God knows the past had presented enormous problems and threats!) in their desire for a successful future. It was difficult, at best, to trust any statement. The past, the historic student "turmoil" of 1989, as Tiananmen was referred to if indeed it was referred to at all, had left on the surface a patina of unreality under which hypocrisy thrived. Everyone wore a mask, smiled, and was superficially pleasant. "Go about your daily work. Pretend nothing unpleasant has ever happened to you" seemed to be the order of the day and, to some of the youngsters, indeed it was. But beneath the surface, where the heart beats, one could sense the seething, the furtiveness and canniness as each one, teacher or student, did everything possible and necessary to achieve one's personal goals. He found himself thinking of Li Jian, who so desperately desired to go to America for "further study," the ubiquitous Ph.D. What a sly cat! He would sell his own mother to achieve his ambition.

He thought of the China he recalled affectionately from more than twenty years ago. When he had first arrived in Shen Shang in 1982, the students had been honest, sincere; marvelous, although academically and culturally starved young people, doing everything they could to realize honest, straightforward ambitions. Hungering for knowledge of the outside world, they had worked unbelievably hard. In cold grey classrooms, in their blue Mao jackets, tight-collared, buttoned to the throat, sitting in strict rows, they had recited their prose, often memorizing large portions of the textbooks doled out to them. Stanley had to smile as he thought of the impossibility of his students in the U.S. coming up to his desk after class to ask for additional homework, as these students did, claiming they needed to work harder to really understand some concept.

Docile? Yes. But more than docile, anxious in those rows of drab communal cloth, willing themselves to acquire knowledge, although not yet able to assert themselves into any of the complexities of the world outside China, their motherland. At that time, the world outside had been denied their generation by the Great Cultural Revolution. The brightest students had thought that Africa, for instance, was a small country south of China, if they thought of it at all. He recalled writing home to his parents for a map of the world, a McNally's official map, so that he could instruct his students in some basic elementary geography.

Today, after almost a quarter of a century later, China had not only emerged into the modern world, but was fast becoming a leader economically and,

Stanley conceded, in time, politically. China, with its billion-plus people, held enormous potential political power on this planet.

China had, like a grand old lady, "opened her doors" to the world. The world had not exactly swept her off her feet. Nor did she want them to, for the masses of China's population, "Socialism with a Chinese flavor" was a superior political and economic system. China's population was not educated to the Freedom of Information Act. Its citizens did not lobby nor vote in a general election. But, in its own way, it was vastly improving the quality of life of China's youth who were having the opportunity to be educated. At the risk of being labeled a socialist, which he certainly was not, Stanley was often heard to tell his students that if it were not for Mao, they would not be sitting in this class in a university today, at least gaining some expectations of their abilities. Maybe one of ten, the child of a Mandarin, would be being privately tutored. The rest would be common peasant laborers in the fields or factories.

To disagree was not to a citizen's advantage; indeed, it could be quite harmful, as prisons full of dissidents attest. In this country, "To each according to his needs" seemed to work well, if on a diminished plane. To Mao's and Marx's credit, the masses were tremendously better off today than they had been not too long ago in China's vast history when a Kuomintang soldier could walk into a crowded movie house and simply shoot a peasant who happened to be sitting in a desirable seat the soldier wanted for himself. "From each according to his ability" was something else. Not unlike countless others in countries in this materialistic world, the "haves" separated themselves from the "have nots" without reluctance, often selling their souls for a jab at TV, a chance to go abroad. These days everyone wanted a slice of the world's pie. The yeast of opportunity among the needy masses was these days generating aggressiveness, and violence, Stanley reflected.

Here in China, the surface docility erupted in sinister and unforeseen ways, the news of which was published as little as possible, of course, as the government imposed heavy censorship. The news of defections was not approved. Nor was that of high-jackings or terrorism. Nor the therapeutic smashing of bottles out of upper story dormitory windows. At times he feared for this ancient dowager sashaying into the brave new world. Dangling an economic carrot, she seduced her own people into latter-day fiefdoms as obsolete as Manchu pigtails. At the same time, she enjoyed a mutual flirtation with the West that sparked what the world called progress.

As he once again changed the position of his pillow and tried to make himself comfortable, Stanley again heard the opening of a door across the corridor. He raised his head and listened. Whispers, light but audible, could be heard from the hallway. Silently, Stanley rose and crept into his living room. He stood at the door, holding his head close to it to catch the sounds.

"I'm scared to death! Be careful! Don't, I tell you, just—" the next words sounded like "bag it!" The next whispers were inaudible. Then the male voice, louder, tense,

"I told you, it's OK! I t-told . . . I t-told you!"

Stanley recognized the voice. At that moment, he recalled too with his linguist's ear that when the student Li Jian became nervous, or his patience began to run out, he was apt to stutter slightly, a not uncommon phenomenon. He was doing this now. Stanley put his ear against the door, the better to hear. He could just follow the young man's words.

"Sl-sleep, *L-Laoshi* Elaine. Go to sleep. I'm ok, ok."

Stanley heard the door of Elaine's apartment being closed. The hallway became very quiet. Well! he thought to himself, Li Jian is now speaking to a teacher of his in a much more familiar manner than one might expect of a student. That could mean only one thing, that their relationship had become more familiar than classroom decorum specified. Very interesting. Or, was it? On the contrary, some of the young foreign teachers in the department, Taylor and Woofy among them, did think it very postmodern to deal on very familiar terms with their students, even to allowing them to address the teachers by their first names. His own position was, that, once a student had been graduated, and continued to communicate with him, he could of course become "Stanley" to that person, observing a rite of passage with which they were both comfortable. As long as he was responsible for a student in a classroom, however, he preferred to be known as Professor Poussaint. He thought of that not as an ego trip, but simply as a necessary maintenance of distance from an over familiarity , especially in a country whose culture was different from the West's, a country that traditionally used first names only in the home, among family, or with close friends.

But what his ears had just witnessed reflected an extremely different situation. Elaine and Li Jian had become close friends? Nothing wrong with that, actually. But what was Li Jian doing in Elaine's room at one o'clock in the morning? There was something rotten in the state of Denmark about that here in China, where such behavior would occasion more than the simple ring of gossip it might have at home. And how had he gotten there in this established, if obviously ineffective, security system?
More interesting, how would he get out? The doors were all locked for the night.

Chapter 22
Sunday Brunch

Although it was some months since a fly had attempted to break and enter the small restaurant off Huang Shan Alley, the shiny blue nylon net screen that fulfilled one of the Ministry of Health's public sanitation requirements remained in place, transforming the early winter sunlight coming through the window into an incandescent glow that enlivened the dark interior. It was a small, typical neighborhood family restaurant. Its eight or ten tables were each covered with blue-and-white checked plastic, scratched and worn from long overuse. A dismal scented odor overhung the room, attesting to one of the kitchen's major breakfast culinary productions, *xiaobing*, deep fried, long doughnuts.

Most of the restaurant's breakfast clients had already eaten their noodles or fried doughnuts and gone off to their routine lives. Business was normally slow of a Sunday morning. From the kitchen, the cook could be heard yelling to his helper which vegetables should be cleaned and readied for lunch. At a table near the cash counter, a couple of unbusy *fuwuyuan* idled with the dial of a tape recorder, erratically blasting the volume against the peeling orange paint on the walls. A waiter in an apron that had not seen the inside of a laundry for some time wiped at the deep-red oilcloth of two unoccupied tables in the center of the small room. At one table against the far wall, a solitary customer added spiced pickle to his dish of boiled noodles, the seemingly unending strands of which he slurped up with zest, occasionally biting through the long strings to enable himself to take a large bite of fried doughnut with his free hand.

At a table along the back wall, Taylor and Wu Fang sat.

Wu Fang played with a bowl of *zhou*, watery breakfast rice, set in front of her. The dish had some time ago cooled in room temperature. She lifted a spoonful of the soupy rice, then flipped the spoon to watch it splatter slowly back into the bowl. The waiter presently walking away from their table had come to ask whether his customers wished to order anything more. Neither one of them heard him.

Wu Fang said, finally, "I wish you'd stop brooding." Taylor grunted as he raised his head ever so slightly from the mug of tea which seemed to be mesmerizing him. He looked bleakly at his wife.

Wu Fang moved her hand across the able to cover his. He made no motion to acknowledge her gesture.

"It's all right, darling. Everything will be all right." She was trying to smile, but the muscles seemed not to be working, neither her own face nor any reaction from his. For the second time that morning, ever since they had awakened and begun to talk with each other about their "problem," she felt her world was about to fall apart.

"You promised me," she tried to continue, but faltered. His look was devastating. It seemed only her youth was reliable, not love, not their future, not the great career they had planned together. Their world was disintegrating, even as they sat there. She could hardly stop the trembling of her body.

Taylor appeared not to notice. She grasped his hand more firmly.

What had he promised during the past few days since she had discovered the horrible romantic affair he had mixed himself up in? When they had lain together in bed a few nights ago, he had pledged that he would stop seeing the woman Xiao Mei. He had sobbed on Wu Fang's breast as he recounted his recent infatuation for the pretty, innocent Chinese student. Yes, he and she had actually planned to run away together. But then Xiao Mei had left the campus so abruptly. One day she had been in his class, attentive in her usual seat; but the next day, she had simply disappeared. He had not seen her since. Her fellow students knew nothing of her whereabouts.

The other night, when Wu Fang had confronted him with her knowledge of his infidelity, he had begged her forgiveness for his childish folly. Woofy was his beloved wife, he insisted; she stood by him. He loved her, he said, Woofy and Taylor would go back to being what they had been to each other. He even made a joke about their being called "the

Bestial Twins." He had agreed they would behave as though this devastating event had never happened, and become again what they had always been, a loving couple, inseparable partners.

In her own mind, Woofy had told herself she would continue to protect him always. She was resolute. Nothing mattered but that she keep Taylor to herself. He belonged to her; he was the other half of her life. By sending away Xiao Mei, she felt she had done what was necessary to insure their own survival and happiness. Now she regarded him with eyes both frightened and fierce. She must win him back. She must achieve control of this situation.

It was safe to assume the student Xiao Mei would not dare to return to the campus or the university town. Wu Fang had made her threats plain enough. It was also clear Taylor knew nothing of the woman's pregnancy. Wu Fang had carefully destroyed that letter, the one she had had the good fortune to happen upon in Judith Treadway's apartment. God was certainly on her side of what was right! Taylor would never know, there was no need for him ever to know, what a very narrow escape their happiness had risked.

She felt a surge of relief as she lovingly admired the top of Taylor's blond head of hair. Everything would be all right, she told herself. Just give it a little time.

They sat like that, her hand on his, a desolate portrait frozen in time, for many minutes. After a long while, he began to speak. What he said gripped her with fear.

"You don't understand." His voice was barely loud enough for her to hear him. She felt as though she were trapped in a box, with sound bouncing back and forth in and around her head. He was saying, "I must see her. I must know that she is all right." When he looked up and as Wu Fang stared into his face, she saw a hard maleness she had never before noticed in the square, chiseled line of the forehead and cheekbone. He frightened her with his pallor. She began to tremble again. Tears of anger and dismay crowded the corners of her eyes.

But she would not give into this whim of his. That is what it was, a whim. She had managed the entire matter so successfully! Until last night he had not mentioned Xiao Mei in two weeks. She had begun to feel relief. The bitch was gone, back to her village. She, Wu Fang, had taken care of that. Then yesterday he had become morose again. Why was he thinking of the girl? Why would he not forget the girl!

The mood at the table broke.

"NO!" she let the word explode in the air before she could master herself.

"No?" He looked at her, as though bewildered. Then a sudden smirk appeared on his face. He drew back, as though he knew a secret.

She withdrew her hand from his, slowly, but aware that she must try hard to control herself.

"We agreed. . . you . . .wouldn't~" she said slowly, mustering a soft voice that was almost a whisper.

"YOU agreed." He accented the "you." "I never agreed to anything." He looked down again into the brownish liquid in the mug in front of him. He picked up the teaspoon beside the mug on the table and began to stir the tea, so vigorously some of the liquid went flying onto the checkered blue-and-white plastic tablecloth. "Now she's disappeared," he said, "and I'm worried."

"She hasn't disappeared!" Her voice became sharp. As he looked up at her, she corrected herself saying in a lower, gentle voice,

"I mean, she's gone quickly home, or something. . . she's a sensible person, she knows what is best—"

Despite her effort, her voice immediately went into a high shrill pitch. "She doesn't WANT you! Don't you understand? Besides, we don't know where she is!"

Her angry tones spread over the little restaurant. A few customers at other tables were staring up from their noodles.

"I don't believe that," he said. "I think she told someone where she was going. Some of the foreign teachers have her in class. Maybe she told one of them where she was going."

He sounded desperate. Her instincts told her he really meant to try to find her. Wu Fang felt a bad queasy sensation in her belly. She was going to be sick. The two spoonfuls of congee she had swallowed earlier heaved in her stomach. She felt weak, hysterical. She looked around the room, but recalled there was no john in this little restaurant.

"I'll be back." She managed to get up, holding hard at her mouth. She fled toward the bluish-bright sunlight at the front of the restaurant, and went out the door. She badly needed to vomit. Where could she find a public toilet? She leaned against a wall to steady herself. She looked around, started for the back of the building.

Inside the restaurant, Taylor hung his head in his hands, elbows hard against the tabletop. Two waitresses idling at the front table giggled and gossiped, turning to look at the tall foreigner at the back of the restaurant, he who had been quarreling so vigorously with the Chinese woman. They thought he was very handsome. He looked so sad! It was romantic to watch a foreigner have a love quarrel with a Chinese woman. The restaurant was very boring until more lunch customers would begin to come in. The waitresses played a few more of the CDs from the stack the manager kept at the counter to give the restaurant a nice prestige in the neighborhood. The cook shouted out again from the kitchen, and one *fuwuyuan* jumped up and ran into the kitchen. She returned struggling with a large basin of raw potatoes splashing in water along with two big kitchen knives.

The three restaurant workers peeled and cut the potatoes into slivers of the right size for stir-frying, a specialty of the restaurant. Then they prepared the long green beans, cleaning and stringing them, then snapping and flinging them into an enamel basin in the center of the round table at which they sat. Next, they began to roll and fill the popular meat and vegetable pork dumplings the foreigners called "pot stickers."

The blond-haired foreigner at the back of the restaurant had cradled his arms on the table and rested his head on them. He seemed to be asleep. They turned the music down, being polite not to disturb him.

When Wu Fang returned, she was silent and pale. She touched Taylor on the shoulder as she sat down opposite him at the little table. He jerked his shoulders at her touch, and raised his head as though abruptly forced out of a long nightmarish dream. He shook his head, as though trying to wake himself from sleep. His eyes were red-rimmed. He said, his voice shaking a little,

"You found a john?"

The restaurant had begun to fill up with luncheon customers. A family of four, a young mother and father with their small son and an old granny, probably the mother of one of the couple, had come in and were enjoying lunch at a nearby table. The little boy bobbed happily on his stool as he stuffed his mouth from a plate of fried, caramelized bananas.

Wu Fang said,

"Darling, shall we have something to eat now? You haven't eaten. It's lunchtime." She was calm now.

"I don't want anything to eat."

"Have some stir-fried potatoes. They're so good here. You love them."

"I don't WANT any stir-fried potatoes."

"Have some."

"Woofy, will you shut up!" He struggled to his feet like a drunken man, then strode forward to the counter to pay the bill. He distractedly patted the pockets of his jacket and trousers to find his wallet, then held it open for the *fuwuyuan* standing at the cash drawer, indicating she take from the wallet for him the money owed, as though he had no idea, or couldn't care less, about what to pay.

Wu Fang stood to the side, neither interfering nor offering to help. As they left the restaurant, she walked silently and docilely just behind her husband, like a good old-fashioned Chinese wife. Once in the street, she took his arm, hurrying with him to the corner, where the bus that would take the Bestial Twins back to the university stood waiting.

Chapter 23
Bureaucratic but Indispensable

On Monday morning at exactly one minute before nine, a Russian-made black sedan without markings drove up to the entrance of the Foreign Guest House. Chief Inspector Ling Feng of the Central Prefecture stepped from the near seat of the automobile as another police officer emerged from its far side, both men simultaneously slamming closed their doors. The driver, in a military cap with a visor sitting tall, did not turn his head, but drove immediately off to the parking lot.

Stanley stood on the stairs near the outer doorway. He needed some fresh air before going inside to attend the command performance meeting the Waiban, the Foreign Affairs Office, had called earlier that morning. He was still in shock from the fact of the killing of Judith Treadway yesterday morning.

Seeing Chief Inspector Ling Feng get out of the car, he moved to greet his good acquaintance from the Central Police Force, then immediately stopped himself, cognizant of public protocol. As Li Feng passed him on the stairs, the two men acknowledged each other with a brief glance into each other's eyes, and a nod of the head. They'd talk later.

The two police officers continued up the stairs to the top where Yang Youli, Director of the Waiban and his deputy waited at the building's entrance to greet them, as protocol demanded. The men stood talking for a few minutes, then went inside, the officials and staff of the Waiban deferentially escorting the honored Chief Inspector and his deputy up the stairs to the Foreign Affairs Conference Room on the second floor. Stanley, who had come inside, wondered why they had elected not to take the elevator. He surmised it was because there were quite a few of them, several of the lower bureaucratic functionaries of the Waiban trailing the officers like a rogue cortege. The police group looked brisk and polished, as though they had donned new uniforms for a special occasion. It *was* a special occasion, a sad and frustrating one. Who would want to kill Judith, one of the most compassionate, kind persons he'd ever met?

A personal vendetta? Hardly. A faculty member who was angry, or jealous of her? Perhaps that young woman teacher who liked to argue with her over women's rights, and other academic or personal matters? What about Li Jian, the student who had lost his scholarship to America because she refused to allow him to cheat. One of his own colleagues? Or a hooligan who had found his way into the university to burgle on a Sunday morning?

All unlikely possibilities for murder in this quiet, academic community. But *someone* had killed Judith Treadway.

In the past few years, Stanley Poussaint, as the US Embassy's representative in this provincial outpost of Beijing, had worked with Inspector Ling Feng on such matters of joint national interest as drug-related issues, cases involving so-called "business people," or hippies who came to town to meet students and sell them pot or cocaine, or the ecstasy tablets. He had been asked to deal with overzealous con boys and young women who felt China a good place in which to swindle or proselytize the local innocents who appeared safe and protected from worldly sophistication. But murder?

Trying to keep his nerves calm and mind clear in the face of his colleague's death, Stanley mounted the stairs to the conference room, walking just behind the Russian foreign experts' contingent which had arrived together in a noisy body, grumbling at the command order to attend this special meeting, a disturbance to their morning's class schedules.

Upstairs, just outside the conference room, the Chinese officials stood in the hallway, speaking in low tones, rare for a conversation in Chinese. Stanley went on into the conference room.

One half of the large meeting hall had been cordoned off recently by the use of plastic louvres, which diminished the vast room, itself reminiscent of the Russian architecture of the 1950's, to a more manageable size. Nevertheless, the cavernous interior and high ceilings were intimidating. In such surroundings, human beings easily became miniscule.

Stanley found himself thinking how he always felt like
an ant when in Tiananmen Square or the People's
Great Hall in Beijing, a reaction that was no doubt
what was intended by the builders. In medieval times,
the ruling class had accomplished getting man down
to manageable size with great cathedrals; in modern
times, political rulers here accomplished the same
purpose with huge secular spaces architected in what
Stanley liked to call "Contemporary Monolith." In
another vein, as he raised his head to observe the
amazing shapes and kinds of chandeliers and side
lamps that decorated these premises designed to
delight foreigners, he reflected that the effect achieved
was of being in a colossal, surrealistic electrical outlet.

Taking a seat at the rear of the large meeting
room, he listened to overhear what Yang Youli and
Chief Inspector Ling Feng and their subordinates, still
standing at the back of the hall but within hearing
distance, were speaking about how they meant to deal
with the shocking event of Professor Treadway's
murder yesterday forenoon.

At about seven-thirty on this Monday
morning, the foreign teachers had received a
telephone call from the Waiban, requesting that they
assemble in the meeting room by nine o'clock, no
later. Now a large group huddled in their seats like
refugees, subdued, hardly speaking. The news of
Professor Treadway's murder had traveled fast. Last
evening the corridors had buzzed with talk, as small
groups of the foreign students gathered in the

passageways to exchange information and grapevine dispatches, waylaying faculty who emerged from other teachers' rooms trying to gather information, or simply to gossip. By now, significant rumors had spread: hooligans were said to have burglarized several campus offices. A disgruntled teacher had killed Professor Treadway. . . A foreign student from the Russian Department had been seen in the English Department wing of Main Building on Sunday morning at the time the murder took place.

The foreign students were being assembled in a separate group this morning. Now, Stanley noted, the foreign experts and teachers waited and watched expectantly to hear what the police would say.

Elaine Tryst leaned back against the sofa on which she sat, one arm protectively around the shoulders of Shelby Johnson who, red-eyed, was sobbing into a Kleenex. Despite some sedation given by the university doctor the previous night, she was still experiencing mild hysteria at intervals since she had discovered the body. The German teacher sat with a book in her lap, pretending to read, but actually watching the police in the doorway. The three Japanese experts sat together, speaking in a low continuous cacophony. Wu Fang and Taylor rested side by side, his arm around her, her hand nervously squeezing his thigh. Next to them, the two Russian women experts sat with dignity, hands clasped in their laps, looking frightened. Stanley felt in his jacket pockets for a package of cigarettes, extracted one, and lit it. The Japanese decided to smoke, nodding and bowing to each other as they found matches and moved a standing ashtray to where it was easily accessible to each of them. To a Japanese, even lighting and smoking a cigarette required teamwork, Stanley thought to himself. How could one of them ever be suspected of planning and executing a murder?

Finally, Director Yang and Chief Inspector Ling Feng moved into the room, followed by the second-ranking police officers. The Chinese officials seated themselves at the front of the room, their chairs facing the foreigners. The official interpreters meanwhile had placed themselves just behind the chairs of each national group, as was the custom, and, as Director Yang began to speak, the murmur of simultaneous translation raised the decibels in the room to a resonant buzz.

Speeches were being made. The Director of the Foreign Affairs Unit expressed the University's deep grief and concern over the untimely death of one of Shi Da's finest foreign experts. The University was dismayed that such an occurrence could take place.

"The Director wishes," the interpreter intoned, "to convey the condolences of his President and all officials of the University colleagues and countrymen of the beloved professor. It was a tragedy that placed a–" The interpreter hesitated a moment. "Ah~" (he was heard to check with the Russian interpreter in the row behind) "placed a BLOT on the lives of everyone in the community. The malefactor will be caught. The President trusts," the interpreter droned on, "that each person would continue to do his duty until this dreadful crime is solved."

As Director Yang spoke, Stanley watched Chief Inspector Ling Feng look carefully over the small, anxious assembly, meticulously examining each individual, as though the group together constituted a fruit stand of fresh mangoes, the ripest of which he was preparing to pluck out and eat.

"~and finally," Director Yang's interpreters explicated, "I also beg each expert and teacher of you to resume at your work as we pursue the difficult task of apprehending the criminals. They *will* be apprehended!"

"Meanwhile," the interpreter's voice along with those of other languages, having risen to the high decibels by now, "You have nothing to be fearful. No! We shall investigate each one of you!"

Translations of Chinese into English, particularly in the boondocks, could be amusing, thought Stanley, if this were not so tragic an event. Wu Fang was seen to bump Taylor's knee hard with her own. Shelby sniffed loudly. The younger of the Russian teachers became caught up in a rapid verbal exchange with the elder of the other two experts. One of them was weeping loudly.

"I have one timely request," Director Yang was saying through the interpreter. "In your view of responsibility and loyalty to the University, we would appreciate it if you all will regard this affair as confidential . . . Please do not speak of this matter outside of the University campus."

Of course, reflected Stanley, the University would be foremostly concerned with its reputation. Understandable. However, there was no keeping a matter like this secret. It must be all over town by now. In this vast country, neither newspaper censorship nor a ban of news on television prevented any community matters of interest from spreading quickly from Beijing to Guangzhou by that simplest, most effective of all means of communications, word of mouth, "the bamboo telegraph."

"We all share the misfortune of Professor Treadway's death. It is not a reflection on the University, nor on China. It is a reflection only on one person, one *criminal*. The police will find out." The interpreter hesitated, then raised his voice to a new pitch, "we will FIND HIM OUT."

When he had finished speaking, everyone began to file out, looking constrained. "God, what a terrible thing to happen!" wailed Shelby as she walked slowly out of the room. "What a tragedy!" Wu Fang agreed with her, shivering. Even she seemed moved by the turn of events.

Just ahead of her, Elaine fluttered her eyelids and smiled at a tall Russian who gallantly stepped aside to allow her to precede him out the door.

Chapter 24
A Bird Flies

On Monday afternoon, as the bell for two o'clock class finished ringing, Stanley rose from his desk in the senior classroom, and went to the blackboard. The class of junior English majors enrolled in his linguistics class sat silent and passive, hands for the most part folded on the desktop, faces expressing only a solemn inscrutability as they waited for their foreign professor to begin to speak. It was doubtful they had not heard of the tragedy yesterday morning, but not a single reaction was being evidenced in the classroom.

"Attention was attracted by a big building lying in the middle of the campus." Stanley rapped his stick against the blackboard. At this morning's meeting with the police, Chairman Zhang had especially solicited the faculty's cooperation in continuing to hold classes in the orderly and methodical manner to which the students were accustomed. Even so, some of them seemed more glassy-eyed than usual. Any personal emotions they might feel about Professor Treadway, who had been a teacher of theirs also these past months, was hidden behind that mask Stanley had come to identify with China and the Chinese. This morning, he had spent a considerable part of the past hour trying to explain to his class in linguistics why the particular syntactical construction in English of "a big building lying in the middle of the campus" was a sentence a reader might think of as comical rather than serious.

The students were about as able to discover humor or error in such a sentence as they would be likely to find a teardrop in the sand. A few of the more responsive students offered wide, bright smiles to let the foreign professor know they were aware he was trying to explain something to them. At least those few were participating. But, for the most part, this class reminded Stanley of the fish bowl in his apartment. A cluster of solemn-eyed blank stares, half-open mouths gaped up at him. Standing at the podium, lecturing on the devices and deviousness of words, as he had done every Tuesday, Thursday, and Saturday afternoon of his adult life, it seemed, he not infrequently felt a manic urge to put his thumbs to his temples, stick out his tongue, and wiggle his fingers in the classic gesture of ape-edness. Gad! They were exasperating sometimes, these kids.

The junior class was especially numbly silent. The seniors, having had a year of foreign teachers, and, in these modern times, were a little more accustomed to responding individually in a classroom. Almost all were absolutely terrified of being called upon to answer a question. On hearing his name called, a student would leap out of his chair, frequently sending books and papers sprawling to the floor. Then, hands stiff at his sides, face turning red as sheets of perspiration appeared at his forehead, in a barely audible voice he could be heard to choke over a few words.

On the other hand, group recitation went quite well. Oh, how they loved it. "Repeat after me," Stanley would say, "Repeat after me. . ." and they would echo his words with such gusto the walls would tremble "med-i-ta-tion, as-sim-i-la-tion;" rapping out each syllable with joyous abandon. "Mary had a lit-tle lamb."

Chairman Zhang claimed he could hear the students chanting from his office at the far side of the building. But, ask of them to state one syllable solo and the earth fell apart.

Stanley knew very well that some of his students disliked him. Probably some of them had decided to their satisfaction that it was he who had murdered Professor Treadway. Often, as he sat at his desk with the door of the classroom open as he waited for the students to come in, he could hear their whisperings in the corridors, the *ji-ji ja-ja* that sounded like bird twitterings. They were unaware that he was listening, and could have been embarrassed to learn that their foreign English teacher understood everything they said in Chinese. Competent in Mandarin, he nevertheless refused, as a matter of principle to allow it to be used in his classes of university students whose major was English. He considered it a crutch. These juniors still in their first weeks of work with him had yet to learn with a shock that the foreign teacher spoke their own native languages with skill and understanding.

These students seemed either to fear him or giggle at him behind his back—a little of both, he supposed—the laughter at least partially a release from their undefined fear of what to them was a new experience: the foreign professor. To his face, of course, they showed absolute respect. As a general rule, he taught his classes as though he were accustomed to conversing with people who knew what he was talking about. He was apt to treat lack of comprehension as a direct attack to the flanks of civilized behavior, and react with bad temper. It took these junior class students time to get used to him. Despite this and other eccentricities—or, perhaps, because of them—he was regarded as an excellent teacher, who numbered several brilliant scholars among his former students.

He looked around his classroom at the students laboring now at their desks over a ten-minute written exercise he had assigned them. Serious faces and frowns emerged, and the pulling at strands of their hair by several of the girl students. The young men were inclined to tap pencils or to pick at their ears. He knew that among the less brilliant as well as the brightest, he had his stalwart supporters. Judith had teased him last year about one of his devoted scholars from whom he had received a note when he was about to go off on leave to Japan for summer vacation. A shy, third-year student's carefully handwritten note to her professor was delicately phrased:

> "My beloved Professor,
>> It was very difficult to meet you! It is sad to part
>> You! It is now I taste the flavor of leaving.
>> Shall we meet again? Whether? When? Where?
>> Next year, I look forward. Please come back soon."

He treasured that letter and a few others like it, unsentimental bastard though he thought of himself.

The evenings he had spent with Judith were among his most pleasant times here on campus. Not that those evenings were not erratic. One never knew when to expect a knock at the door, a student visit. Judith was kinder and more patient than he about such domestic interruptions. He preferred his evenings with her to be private, a peaceful few hours of companionable talking and reading, along with a relaxing drink, or some tea. Interruptions dismayed his sense of privacy.

She had sometimes teased him about being in China too long without a break; he became easily angry, a little paranoid. Was he as temperamental as others claimed? Or simply just as precise and demanding of his friends and students as he was of himself. He could not tolerate laxity in anyone. He prided himself on being a person who, if called upon, could within five minutes, put his hands on an illustration of Sisyphus and give a respectable account of myth, context and background.

Looking about the room at the students engrossed in their work, he took particular notice of the female student called Xiao Mei, whom Taylor Battle was said to have been interested in lately. She was reportedly pregnant, Judith had confided to him just last Saturday evening, during what was sadly to be their last meeting together. So the girl was still in class? She had not gone away from the university? Judith, in the brief conversation they had held about Taylor and his involvement with the young woman, had given him the impression she had left for the countryside. But there she was, sitting toward the back of the classroom studiously writing in her notebook. From time to time she looked up as though she were carefully thinking about his lecture and noting important points. But her face bore no expression, neither of interest, boredom or any other discernible emotion. For the second time in an hour, he found himself impressed by the great talent of the Chinese for donning the mask of impassivity, whether it was out of a lack of response to what might normally excite interest, the endurance of pain, or a simple ignorance of consequence.

As the class began to dismiss at the passing bell, and she walked forward to the door, Stanley called out her name, "Wang Xiao Mei!"

The girl jumped, startled.

He walked slowly toward the door, making certain the other students had departed. Then he faced her.

"I thought you had left the university."

She said nothing, her face unsmiling and unresponsive as she stood there. She might not have understood him.

"I thought you were going—" he began to say "to the country," but stopped as he realized this was possibly too personal an inquiry, an intrusion into a matter with which he would not normally concern himself. Before he could say more, she whispered, in a voice so soft he had to bend close to her to catch the words, "Tonight, *Laoshi*. The train goes tonight." Then she had stepped ahead of him out of the doorway and was scurrying down the stairs.

He was quite certain she must know about Professor Treadway's death. The student monitor said the news had spread over the campus like a bush fire, despite the administration's efforts to keep it quiet. Yet she gave no indication of awareness or interest in any personal matter beyond the academic confines of the classroom, excepting for the murmured information about her leaving.

She might have been a visitor from Mars, Stanley thought, as the girl turned at the corner of the stairs, her eyes dark as a frightened deer's in that otherwise pale, flat face.

Chapter 25
Old Eyes See Everything

Dressed in ordinary trousers and a plain *mao* jacket, which many middle-aged and elderly Chinese still favored, Chief Inspector Ling Feng blew on his hands and turned a corner past the Arts Building. He, Ling Feng, did not often conduct routine legwork. That's what his detectives were for. But the Treadway case was a delicate one, involving a foreigner. All attention must be given to its quick and accurate solution. It was for this reason that he had spent the past cold hour of this Monday afternoon personally walking about the campus of Shi Da in the cold, talking with caretakers, gatekeepers and doorkeepers, vendors, service people, *fuwuyuan*, anyone who conceivably had a function on or about the university grounds, and who might have noted something unusual yesterday morning.

Now he found himself at Xiao Men, "Little Gate," which opened into a lane off the northeast corner of the campus. Actually, Xiao Men was little more than a large hole in the brick wall. It had been created over a period of time by students prising out bricks until now the opening was large enough for both walkers and students riding bikes to negotiate. Using this exit from campus rather than Da Men, "Big Gate," the University's main entrance, represented a considerable saving of time for those students traveling north off campus, or getting to the public bus transportation just a few yards away from where the lane swung into a main avenue. The corner was also a convenient location from which to flag a cruising taxicab.

Today, in mid-November, the little lane was frozen and bumpy, rutted with the tracks of bicycles and carts that had used it in milder, muddy weather. Here and there, small mounds of dirty, encrusted snow lay at the sides of the narrow dirt road. As Ling Feng came through the gate, an oncoming student adroitly braked, dismounted and stepped aside, making way for the older man. Ling Feng nodded acknowledgment of the courtesy.

On sunny days, a dozen vendors could be found on this corner, selling everything from sweet-smelling pork buns, *baozi*, to pens, fruits, chewing gum, roasted ears of corn on the cob, and even a few illegally-gotten watches to be disposed of cheap to a student with a few extra *yuan*. But this morning the lane was almost deserted.

"*Nihao, Laodaye!*" "Hi, old uncle!" Ling Feng called out as he approached an elderly man squatting on a wooden box in front of a bicycle resting upside down on its seat with its handlebars on the ground.

"Su Wen," the old man replied after Ling Feng had shown a badge and asked his name. Ling Feng recalled the man had been cooperative with one of his detectives in an earlier case involving a student. The old man supported his wife, the Inspector knew, plus his old mother, and widowed daughter with a child, all on the few *fen* he received from repairing mostly students' bicycles. Day in and day out, he was a fixture of Xiao Men. Many of the local day students rode their bicycles to and from the University daily, come rain or snow, and depended on the old man to keep their transportation in running condition.

Su Wen gave a bicycle spoke a deft twist to get it back into place, methodically straightened it out with a pair of pliers, and tossed the small wrench back into a tin box of tools lying on the frozen ground. He gave the wheel a spin, then leaned to check its alignment with a careful eye. He appeared to be thinking. Only then did he answer the question Ling Feng had put to him a moment ago.

"*Henduoren shang chuzuche*, many people get into taxis," he replied to the police inspector. He elaborated. "Well, three or four, perhaps. Yesterday morning?" The old man continued to look at the wheel he was repairing as he listened to Ling Feng's description and questions.

"And were you here yesterday morning, *Laodaye*?" The old man laughed. His eyes were tearing from the cold. His nose was leaking snot. He turned to blow his nose toward the ground, the force causing the snot to make a small neat hole in the snow. "I am always here!"

Ling Feng asked him another question.

"Yes, sir. Certainly, sir. I try to keep my eye on everyone coming in or going out, sir."

Ling Feng observed the old man's hands, red and calloused, the skin cracked. Those were hands that suffered a lifetime of manual labor without the luxury of gloves. The nails were fissured and discolored. This old bicycle repairman spent most of his life out here on this spot, in all kinds of weather. "As long as they can ride 'em, sir, I can fix 'em," he was saying.

He removed his worn cap, and scratched at his head. He seemed to be thinking about the last question Ling Feng had asked him.

Finally, looking out toward the main street, he nodded. "*Yi-ding!*" "Yes. Certainly. No doubt about it." Yesterday morning he had seen a person matching the description the Inspector had just given him come rapidly through Xiao Men and get into a taxi.

"Are you sure about the clothing?"

Su Wen nodded his head affirmatively and broke into an open smile, pleased with his own memory. He tapped the side of his skull with an index finger. "*Wode danao bucuo!*". . . My head works well!"

A sudden wind blew chill. These early winter winds from off the Gobi Desert were cruel. Grey skies. The old man's breath gusted out of his mouth to float off in steamy wisps into the icy air as he described the person he had seen run hurriedly through the campus gate, flag down a taxi, and rush off.

"*Ta huanghuang zhangzhang de!*" He blew out his cheeks. "Very excited and nervous." He remembered the taxi was a red color, a small car. No, of course he had not gotten the number. As he replied to the question, Su Wen suddenly faced Ling Feng with hostility in his voice. Why should he take down numbers of taxis that students got into? That was not his job. He was not a spy, sir. As a citizen, he was happy to help, but this was not the Cultural Revolution, sir. . .

Ling Feng pressed no further inquiries. Besides, he had the information he wanted. He patted the old man on the shoulder to placate him. "*Meiyou wenti, meiyou wenti!*" "No problem!" It would be easy enough to find the taxi driver. There were only a few red taxis in the town. All taxis were registered, along with their drivers, by both the Ministry of Transportation and the Central Police.

The smell of sweet potatoes being roasted over charcoal caused Ling Feng's nostrils to twitch. He realized he was both hungry and cold. He walked the few steps to where a sweet potato vendor leaned over an oil drum that had been converted into a charcoal brazier. A young woman in a thick wool sweater and with a scarf tied in the Russian babushka style over her head, turned the sweet-smelling potatoes on the grill over the fire, as she called out, "*Kaodigua! Kaodigua!*". . . "Hot sweet potatoes!" The vendor's cries reminded him of a saying of his mother's that he recalled from childhood: as long as the street vendors cried out their wares, it was not really winter yet. In deep cold, those street sellers brave or desperate enough to remain out of doors muffled their mouths and noses, letting the sight and smell of their wares speak for themselves. Nevertheless, today it was damned cold. . .

"*Zhe liang ge*" . . . "These two," said Ling Feng, pointing to two large potatoes roasting on the brazier. The woman handed him the two hot potatoes as he placed a one-*pyuan* note in her hand. He walked back to the old man at the bicycle, and held out a potato.

"Here, old man," he said, "get warm."

The bicycle repairman raised his head from the brake he had been testing and twirling. He took the potato from Ling Feng while continuing to concentrate on the wheel.

"*Zhe-ge bucuo!*" he announced, hardly looking up. "Hot potatoes not bad! Not bad at all! *Ting hao!*" he murmured to no one in particular, setting the potato on top of the tools of his wooden tool box until he was satisfied that the smooth results of his twirling of a loose brake pedal meant it was in good and safe running order. Only then did he pick up the steaming potato from the top of his workbox and bite into it. But Ling Feng was not unaware of the oh-so-slight deferential bow the old man made toward him as the police inspector strode back onto the campus and toward the main gate. Old habits die hard, even in the most reformed of societies.

Chapter 26
Alibis and Visitations

"Well, I think I have covered most of the bases," Inspector Ling Feng remarked to Stanley Tuesday afternoon as they sat together in the Inspector's office at the Central Police Station. Actually, what he said to Stanley in Mandarin translated literally as "I have stood on all four corners." But the two men understood each other's idioms without awkwardness.

"I have questioned each of the foreign experts, including yourself," he smiled at Stanley, "and the younger teachers, one by one. I have my men verifying all alibis. We will be ready to order a meeting tonight." Stanley realized, as a Chinese, Ling Feng preferred to say nothing more of the situation until the meeting itself, where the full revelations would be spelled out.

"You have certainly done a commendable amount of work in a very short time," Stanley replied in his excellent Mandarin. He offered the Chief Inspector a cigarette from his pack of Double Worlds, and the two men relaxed back in the chairs. Inspector Ling Feng leaned back in his chair to practice blowing a few smoke rings, a trick Stanley had taught him on one of their early meetings years ago. The two men had worked together in the past on several matters

207

involving security questions in the foreign community. Stanley, as the eldest continuous resident expert, was not new to being consulted by the local police on matters regarding the safety or other concerns of his countrymen. As the American Embassy's local point man, also, he had the right in certain emergencies (and certainly this was one!) to be informed of certain delicate matters when it came to the welfare of U.S. citizens. As Inspector Ling Feng's friend and sometime-colleague, he was on occasion made privy to other interesting information, although it was well understood between the two what official limitations on revelation of sources there might exist on both sides of the diplomatic fence.

Usually Stanley enjoyed his occasional sorties out of the academic into what he sometimes referred to as the "real world" of security and sleuthing downtown. But his friend and colleague Judith Treadway's death was a far different situation. As he gazed through the dust of the window glass to the street, where busses, trucks and autos of every conceivable make and year since Henry Ford, plus bicycles and mopeds and motorcycles, all threaded dauntlessly around each other along the dusty macadam road in the common daredevil rush hour, he thought about what he knew so far.

That everyone had a confirmable alibi on a quiet Sunday morning threw a certain light on the lack of loneliness in the small community, at least among the foreign members. The Bestial Twins had gone into the center of town on the early Foreigners' Commuter Special bus, and had not returned until late afternoon. Xiao Li, the driver, had checked Taylor and Woofy aboard at eight o'clock in the morning, along with the Japanese and Russian experts and several foreign students riding into town for their weekly shopping. Elaine had also been on the bus, and, although she had gotten off at an earlier stop, the local Christian Church, she had a plethora of witnesses who bore testimony to her being a most vocal member of the evangelical services performed there from nine o'clock until almost noon on Sunday.

Shelby claimed to have slept all that dreadful Sunday morning until her "disastrous noonday sortie" in terms of her discovery of Judith Treadway's body. She had a compelling alibi to back her up. Wei Ping, the *fuwuyuan* on duty at her desk not fifty feet from the door of Shelby's flat on the fourth floor of the Foreigners' Guest House, was certain teacher Johnson had not emerged all morning. As was her habit of weekends, the teacher had placed the red "Do Not Disturb" notice on her outer door handle late Saturday night. It was there until just before Wei Ping went off duty late Sunday morning. At that time, teacher Johnson had opened the door, emerging in her bathrobe with her empty thermos bottle, which Wei Ping had taken from her to fill with hot drinking water from the electric vat down the hall. She had then carried it into the teacher's apartment and set it on the floor in the kitchen, where the foreign teacher was cooking eggs. Wei Ping had gone into the teacher's bedroom to make up the bed. Then she went off to her home.

Stanley, as well as the other foreign experts and teachers, was of course technically also under suspicion. He had spent the morning absorbed in one of his beloved Ouspensky texts, while a favorite Beethoven quartet played softly in the background. Unfortunately none of that aesthetic provided a realistic alibi of one's physical whereabouts.

By luck, he had recalled that his telephone had rung at about ten o'clock that morning, a fact that resulted in his verbal thrashing of a senior student for intruding upon his Sunday morning privacy. The student, after an initial denial of making the call, due to simple, naïve embarrassment and "Chinese modesty," had admitted that indeed it was he who had disturbed Professor Poussaint on a beautiful Sunday morning, and been "*pi-pinged*," criticized, for it by the professor over the telephone. The following day, the student had made a special trip to the professor's office to apologize, and to beg forgiveness for his great fault. He left Stanley's presence a thoroughly confused young man, after being profusely thanked by the professor for having disturbed him when he did on Sunday morning. The police had not explained to the student why they were interrogating him to verify his Sunday call. He had returned to his dormitory in a state of partial confusion and anxiety.

"Oh, it was good, *taihaola*, for you that the bold student telephoned you Sunday morning, Professor Poussaint, or you might be in dire trouble, dear sir!" Inspector Ling Feng ran his thumb competently down the list of University personnel before him on his desk.

Of course, there was a whole campus full of faculty and students who could have plotted and carried out a murder. Well, nonsense! Stanley said to himself. Motive had to be summarily ruled out for all but a very few. What Chinese colleague would murder a foreign expert? Motives for professional reasons appeared too ridiculous to be considered. What possible gain would serve any department member? Chinese colleagues profited, as did students, by Professor Treadway's presence as a consultant to the department, not by her demise.

Although Inspector Ling Feng could not be expected to confide in him completely this early in the investigation, Stanley sensed he leaned toward ruling out a student as the murderer. Conceivably, this could be the work of a hothead. Certainly crimes of violence, committed in moments of rage, often abetted by *baijiu* or other strong liquors, were not uncommon in this strict, controlled university society. But the killing of a foreign teacher by a disgruntled student seemed hardly likely. The risks of absolute and cruel punishment were too great to risk murder. Still, if emotions ran high? Certain students had been extremely upset with the results of the marking of their senior term papers. Which reminded him of something he meant to look into.

Taking his leave of Ling Feng, he hailed a taxi back to the campus. Entering the Foreign Guest House, he dropped off his coat in his room and went out to the corridor. The *fuwuyuan* were not at their desk. It was their dinnertime. He climbed a flight of stairs to the floor of Judith's apartment. The third floor hallway was empty too as Stanley crossed the side corridor, looking to the right and left. There was no one in sight. In front of the doorway to Room 302, he slid the celluloid credit card he held palmed in his right hand through the slit between the door and its frame, manipulating the bolt until he felt the slight release of the lock. He slowly pushed the door, and entered the flat.

Judith's rooms looked undisturbed, although he knew the police had been there earlier to investigate. The room was orderly, as Judith herself had been orderly. Rows of books were arranged neatly on the wooden bookshelf, end to end. An ivy plant in an earthenware pot held upright an assortment of books and pamphlets. Long, flowered nylon drapes of indeterminate beige hung at the sides of the windows. In the center of her desk sat her closed laptop, some stacks of papers neat beside it. He flipped hurriedly through them, finally determining that what he was searching for was not among them.

A glance into the bedroom confirmed that she had not recently used it as a workplace. To him, the room was surprisingly feminine for Judith. Rows of toiletries, some cologne bottles, a brush and comb lined the makeshift dressing table, its wooden surface covered with a pink silk, fringed cloth. On the wall over the table hung an oval mirror he remembered her purchasing during an autumn joint outing to the local free market. A single long, narrow scroll of Tang dynasty calligraphy hung from ceiling to floor level near the bed, which was covered with a silk amber-colored quilt. A functional room, on the whole, but decorated with some attention. He found himself wondering whether she had ever wished to be loved in it.

One window was slightly ajar, letting in a slight draft against the heat of the radiators. He returned to the living room. Outside the window, the sun was setting. A streak of gold crossed the room like a laser aimed at the gray leather couch against the far wall near the door. He knelt on the seat of the couch, bending over the back to look behind it. Wedged between couch and wall was a sheaf of paper. He reached for it, glanced hurriedly at the student essay, then folded and inserted it in the inner pocket of his jacket. As he did so, he heard a scratching sound at the door, and looked over to see the knob turning slowly. Quickly he scrambled away from the couch and placed himself behind one of the long beige drapes, aware he felt a little like Polonius, but relieved he had a place to hide himself quickly.

A figure entered the room and went directly to the desk. There were sounds of muttering and of sifting through the piles of papers. Peeking through the side of the curtain, Stanley could discern only a shadow. He heard an enraged whisper, "*Tamade! Tamade!*" Hands grasped at the papers as though to fling them against the wall. Slowly, however, as though in defeat, the hands replaced the papers in the pile, making an awkward, but successful, effort to approximate the stack as it had rested on the desk. A turn in profile toward the bookshelf, a scurrying to lean against the door as though to detect any sound outside, was followed by the furtive re-opening and closing of the door. The intruder's departure was as swift and smooth as the entrance had been.

Stanley felt himself once again alone in the room. His knees were shaking so hard he could not move readily. Had the interloper entered for what Stanley himself had come in search of? Or something else? It was an unbelievable fluke that he had not been detected behind those thin, semi-transparent drapes. On the other hand, he almost wished he had dared a confrontation; but then he thought better of it. Was he afraid? Well, the idea of having a knife pulled on him was not an appealing one. When angry or violence-prone, many students, as well as other local citizens, armed themselves. Most killings in China were accomplished with knives. Discretion being the better part of valor, he was glad he had remained hidden. What had turned around would come around. A smell of sweat, alcohol and local domestic cigarettes hovered on the air of the room now, despite the draft from the open window.

Chapter 27

A Mystery of Manners

It was almost nine o'clock Tuesday evening when Shelby returned to her apartment from the library. It seemed incredible that it had been only two days since Judith Treadway's murder. It seemed eons ago, somehow, what with all the police and Waiban meetings, and having to talk with the Chinese Chief Inspector of Police himself in between classes. Inspector Ling Feng's English was pretty good. Shelby had told him so, and been rewarded with a very pleasant smile from the usually stern face. He had been very solicitous about her feelings following the murder, appearing not to say anything that would upset her, although he had asked a lot of questions about all the foreigners, even the Russians and the Japanese. She had explained that most of the Americans had little contact with those teachers, as *they* spoke very little English and most of the English-speaking experts and teachers were lucky to know a little Chinese but couldn't be expected to know Russian and Japanese, too!

He hadn't made her go to back to the office she had shared with Judith, which she appreciated. The office was sealed off. She didn't think she ever wanted to go in there again, no matter what!

Two other very polite and friendly police officers had come to call on her early in the afternoon.

They'd offered their condolences, and asked almost the same questions about her relations with her late colleague and with the other teachers as the Chief Inspector had asked, which had been fine, both the relations and the questions. They had then gone away, but left her feeling drained. She had needed to get out of her apartment to work; she felt she would be able to concentrate better and grade some papers required for tomorrow's classes if she were in surroundings less homey and familiar to her than her own flat. Because the library was kept at minimal heat in November, most of its patrons, while reading or conducting their research, continued to wear their overcoats or heavy outdoor jackets indoors. Shelby, snug in the pink anorak she had bought at the Youyi Shangdian, the big Friendship Department Store in Beijing when she first arrived in China in September, was quite comfortable. She had been delighted, if a little surprised, to find such a good-looking polyurethane, fleece-lined ski jacket in a Chinese department store, at less than half the price she would have paid at home for the same article, with its "Made in China" label sewed into the back of the collar.

In the anonymous silence of the library, she was able to force herself to concentrate, and had gotten the entire batch of papers done in short order. It had taken her considerably less time to read through them in the comparatively chill—speaking both literally and metaphorically—atmosphere of the library than it would have taken her in her apartment, where she had a tendency to wander into the kitchen happily and often for a cookie or a cup of hot tea.

As she unlocked her own outer door, the telephone was ringing. She scuttled in, dropping her books and tote bag on the sofa as she passed, hurrying toward the phone. At this hour, it might well be a call from the U.S., from home. The phone bell scratched its message into the air with a jangle that made her shiver.

"*Wei*? Hello?"

It was Elaine. She was crying. She was also angry. "Where the hell have you been? I've been trying to get you all evening!"

Shelby explained about the library, which Elaine seemed not to hear. "All evening I've been trying to get you!" She was near screaming. "I came down to see you, but you weren't there!" There was accusation in her voice, as though Shelby had deliberately not shown up for an appointment.

"Elaine, what's wrong? What can I do for you?" Shelby interrupted, cutting into Elaine's harangue.

"What's wrong?" She was beginning to sob. "My whole life is falling apart, and you ask me, 'What's wrong'?"

"Tell me, tell me, what's going on? Do you want to come down here?"

"No, I don't want to go down *there*!" Coming from almost anyone else, the anger in the voice would be abusive. But Shelby felt she had learned to deal with Elaine's peculiar moods. She asked her, speaking in a cool, level voice,

"Would you like me to come up to your apartment? What is it, Elaine?"

There was a crackle on the other end of the telephone.

"Do as you damn please!" and the phone went into a dead buzz.

Throwing her anorak over her shoulders because the hallway was drafty, she put her keys into a pocket, then remembered to dash into her bathroom, set the plug into place in the tub, and start the hot water for her evening bath running in a thin, scalding trickle. It would take a good hour to fill the tub enough for a decent sitzbath. She pulled her apartment door closed, and went out and up the flight of stairs to Elaine's floor. She lived in Apartment 214, just down the corner from Stanley who was in #211.

The door to #214 was ajar. Shelby knocked softly, then pushed the door open, and walked in. Elaine lay on the sofa, her back toward the room. She wore a grey woolen sweater pulled over a faded brown and yellow Indian print skirt. Her feet were bare.

She gave no sign that she had heard Shelby come into the room. Shelby softly closed the door behind her. Elaine seemed to fade into the sofa, her legs pulled up under her as she hunched like a fetus. Her first words were, "Why have you come here? I have nothing to tell you."

Since the term began, Shelby had already been through a few of these emotional crises with Elaine. A disappointment with a student, a falling out with a Chinese colleague, a flirtation which she indulged in with zest and regularity, come to nothing; Elaine's mood swings were predictable in their unpredictable frequency. She wondered what this problem would turn out to be. She found herself hoping fervently that whatever it was, it had nothing to do with Judith's murder.

She couldn't believe it would have. Elaine was flaky, but certainly not a murderer. Yet she flushed suddenly with uneasiness. She was remembering her father's warnings to her about certain friends through high school: "Who knows what your friends are really capable of? Always look *behind* the obvious – try to figure out the reasons people act as they do." Elaine was certainly looking and acting unhinged. Tired suddenly, Shelby sat down in one of the two armchairs facing the sofa, shaking her shoulders to let the anorak slide off them. Elaine's apartment was comfortably warm.

There was silence in the room. Shelby wondered how, if she did decide to ask Elaine a direct question, she could phrase it. Finally she said, softly,

"Elaine, do you want to talk?" Another minute or two of silence. "Would you like me just to sit here with you?"

Silence. Minutes went by.

"Elaine, we're friends." Shelby stood up and walked closer to the hunched figure on the sofa. "Tell me what's bugging you." Controlling a sudden desire to shake the other woman, yet feeling she should try in some way to establish better contact than the current silent emotional performance allowed, Shelby reached to put a kind hand on the woman's shoulder. Elaine jumped as though a snake had threatened her, and turned to stare up at the ceiling. Her fists were clenched. "Leave me alone!"

"I'm your friend, Elaine." Shelby repeated, as she crouched to sit on the floor beside the couch, keeping space between herself and the now sobbing woman, but edging close enough to see her face, which was turned slightly sideways facing the direction where Shelby sat.

"Do you want to tell me what's wrong?" Shelby asked.

Silence. Shelby tried another tack. She found she could barely get the sentence out. "Elaine, is this about, has it anything to do with~?"

She didn't get to finish, for Elaine burst into a wail. She thrust her legs out and down the length of the couch, then turned her back again against Shelby. She stretched her right arm over the couch, returning to the infant position she had been in when Shelby entered the apartment, curling up her legs again and burying her head into a corner of the gray couch.

Shelby said, "Please, Elaine, will you tell me?" Another interminable few minutes went by.

Then, still fearful for her colleague's well-being but exasperated as well, she said, "Would you like me to leave?" There was still no answer at all.

Shelby looked around the apartment Elaine occupied. Unlike her own, Elaine's quarters were spare, undecorated, consisting of the standard issue Foreign Office furnishings. One couch, two armchairs that reminded Shelby of the furnishings in her grandmother's house when she went to visit her as a little girl almost thirty years ago. One small wooden table, one bookcase. A refrigerator was one of the "three importances" each foreign teacher was issued. (The other two were a washing machine and a television set, the symbols of social status in China.) Elaine had not bothered to move her refrigerator into the kitchen, as Shelby had hers. It remained against a principal wall of the living room, to a western eye looking orphaned and out of place. To a Chinese eye, this new luxury was no doubt quite properly in its position of prominence in a household that could afford such luxury.

A reproduction of a painting of Christ hung against another wall; a cross and a large National Geographic map of China on a third. The room seemed so unlike the bumptious, energetic Elaine Shelby had come to know. Funny, she could remember being in this room only once before, during the week they had first arrived. As far as Shelby knew, Elaine did not entertain any visitors; nor could she recall Elaine's suggesting even that she, Shelby, "drop by" to her room for a purely social visit. Elaine made a habit of popping into Shelby's quarters on the lower floor whenever she had a mind to, which was frequently. Shelby did not really mind. Accessibility by one's colleagues was a price one paid, she supposed, for being on the first floor of a walkup building.

She said again, "Would you like me to leave?"

There was a mumble from the cushions. "I don't want to talk to you. I don't want to talk to anyone. Don't you understand?"

Shelby took the risk of patting the woman's back. Elaine rose up from the couch.

"I said, Don't touch me!" She shrieked the words. "I'm not worthy. . . I don't want to be touched!"

Shelby looked again around the sparsely furnished room. She hadn't noticed near the door, in the tiny hallway, a poster of a Buddha seated in the lotus position, feet crossed underneath, hands in lap, an absolutely benign and peaceful expression on the face. A face of pure happiness.

Elaine screamed, "Just leave me alone! Stop interfering with my life, okay? I'm just fine!"

"Hey, it's okay." Shelby's feelings of concern were being replaced with some of anger and resentment now at being used as a handball for Elaine's histrionics. She felt sorry for her colleague; she was also feeling tired and useless. She was not a policewoman; nor was Elaine allowing her to be a friend or counselor. Why had she phoned? Whatever the problem was, it was one Shelby didn't feel she could be helpful with. Her usual positive and energetic associate had trouble on her mind. In her present mood, it seemed better to leave her alone. She seemed in no immediate danger.

"Elaine, if I can't help you, I'm going to bed now." She pulled herself up from the floor where she had been sitting. Still only silence came from Elaine. Shelby started toward the door.

"Let me know if I can do anything, ok? I'm there for you if you need me. Meanwhile, I'm just going to bed. Ok?" She stood in the doorway, feeling awkward, but reaffirming through Elaine's attitude that she was accomplishing nothing. "Call me, or come down, anytime. Ok?"

"Leave me alone," muttered Elaine. "Just leave me alone. I don't want to talk about it. You just don't understand anything!"

As Shelby was letting herself out of the apartment, Elaine turned on the sofa, and cried,

"Life's so simple for you, isn't it? Fuck you! You never get involved in messes you can't handle. Righteous woman! You would never dream of committing a crime! Fuck you!"

Shelby let herself out, closing the door, and went down to her apartment to get ready for bed. Gad! One made strange friends in a foreign country. She was no longer sure that she understood any part of Elaine. Had she had something to do with the murder? Shelby found that hard to believe, but still, what a weird woman! One minute she was full of ideas and energy, full of gossip. Then, like tonight, she was filled with depression and hysteria. Shelby wished she really had someone to talk with about this situation. She reflected that she and Stanley talked to each other like friends. She really didn't like to gossip, but he seemed like a good person to tell some of her thoughts and frustrations to. Besides, if Elaine were involved in Judith's murder—? It was late now, but she would talk with her tomorrow.

Elaine was always so much on top of everything. She knew all the gossip, every little thing that happened at Shi Da. What had caused her to become so unstrung?

Back in her own apartment, Shelby put a finger into the bath water she had run earlier. It was just the right temperature, good. Since the hot water in the Foreign Guest House was shut off automatically at ten o'clock each evening, or earlier, if the *fuwuyuan* wanted to leave the building and get home earlier. The survival trick here was to run a bathful of scalding water earlier in the evening. By ten o'clock or ten thirty, when one was ready for it, the water was just fine, if occasionally a little rusty.

Shelby threw a few of her favorite bath salts into the water, and relaxed in its quite comfortable warmth, contemplating the encounter. She had just had it with Elaine. What in the world was so disturbing the woman? Granted her sometime friend had a good number of quirks and strange behavior patterns, the exhibition this evening was still bizarre. Well, stay out where you're not wanted, Shelby, she advised herself, as she leaned back in the tub. Elaine had certainly given her marching orders, much as Shelby felt tomorrow might find Elaine in a quite different frame of mind. Maybe she was suffering that Seasonal Acute Depression syndrome, SAD, she'd been reading about in some of the American magazines she received from home. Or maybe she - O God! Shelby drew in her breath sharply, Please not. No, Elaine, never . . .

Out of the tub, she pulled herself into the big, comfy terry cloth robe her mother had just sent her as a pre-Christmas present. Then she moved into the bedroom, where sitting at the edge of the bed, she cut and polished her toenails.

Well, she would see Stanley at lunch tomorrow, if not between classes. They always talked together, just for fun. She'd just tell him about this odd situation.

She had put away her nail clippers, brushed her teeth and was settling into bed when the phone rang. It was eleven o'clock. What?

It was Elaine. "Shelby, I'm so sorry, Shelby! I'm so sorry!" She was sobbing loudly. "Could you come up? Please."

The last word, uttered as a plea, dispelled any hostile or negative reaction Shelby was feeling following this evening's earlier events. Patience, patience. . .

"I'll be right up, Elaine," she said. "Chill out, girl."

Chapter 28
A Poetry Festival

The second annual Poetry Festival of the Foreign Languages Department was being very successful. There had been a considerable number of entries for readings this year, given the presence of foreign students from so many countries. As they had the previous year, participants were permitted to read either from their own poems or a selection from the work of one of their countrymen. On the whole, the results had been an interesting and diverse academic salad. From Pushkin to Pasternak through a modest selection of haiku and kensu from one of the Japanese experts; a good deal of personal free verse from the Canadians and the Americans as well as selections from representative favorites from Robert Frost to Anthony Hecht and Stephen Dunn. The great Tang Dynasty poet Tu Fu had appeared on the printed program as a sort of guest of honor (read of course by one of the outstanding students from the Chinese Department), the host country not about to be outdone by foreign writers. Poems in Chinese written by some of the foreign students excited great enthusiasm and admiration. It was far from easy to master the Chinese language well enough to write acceptable poems in it, as Stanley Poussaint remembered well from his own modest past efforts. Other forms filled out the roster, including not a few innocent parodies from some of the younger students who found it easier to imitate the greats than to strike out creatively on their own.

For this literary occasion, the ballroom was illuminated by the hundred or so overhead plastic light fixtures secured from the ceiling or fixed as wall chandeliers. The lights certainly succeeded in decorating the huge ballroom by daylight: it looked rather like a gala electric supply store display. The sound system was quite good. Well-positioned microphones enabled the various poets and poetasters to speak from their own places at the large round tables rather than having to walk to the far stage. This innovation lent a pleasant informality to the occasion.

Taylor Battle was not one of those who had put on the line a claim either to authorship or expressed appreciation of poetic forms. Nor was he sitting at the same table as his wife, but rather at one farther down the room. Morose and apparently sulking, he had not spoken to anyone since the poetry fest began. Some Russians at the same table as he had at first made an effort to include him in the festivities, raising their glasses toward him during the general toasts to the participants' health and success. But in the wake of his evident lack of interest in their company, they had withdrawn their efforts and left him to himself. Most of the time he stared fixedly at his wife's back, as though willing Wu Fang to turn and look at him. For her part, she seemed to be having a hilarious time, laughing and calling out toasts to the group of mostly male foreign students at the table at which she appeared to preside. No one would think it strange that The Bestial Twins sat at separate tables on an occasion of this sort. From their arrival at the beginning of the term, they had made their pursuit of "independent choices" and individuality in their academic and social choices clear to anyone who would listen.

Not surprisingly, Wu Fang had chosen to read several of her own long poems. Her subject matter was predictable, but not uninteresting. Didactic, she appeared at times to be reading a speech rather than a poem. Her sinuous verbal segues attempted to demonstrate that Asia was superior to the West, and

"Asians must awaken to their true significance!
Take to the helm of our ship!
Refuse to condone Western power!"

Her voice had that strident energy that makes people stop talking and listen. She ended with an exhortation to women to "cast off the male yoke," which the poet symbolized as "masculine Western culture suffering in confrontation with the true feminine power of the Eastern Hemisphere." Enthusiastic clapping, particularly from the fawning admirers at her own table, greeted her. But then, most participants had their own private cliques, whom they invited or cajoled to be certain to be on hand as claques.

Even as the next poetry reader was announced, the audience had begun to stir and move about, as

Chinese audiences do without compunction during a long program. Some of the guests were occupied in their own conversations, not out of deliberate rudeness, but in what was a classical local cultural response during a prolonged presentation of any kind. Old China hands claimed they never quite became accustomed to the habit of the members of a Chinese audience moving about freely and talking quite loudly during a performance (one Westerner had never got over his shock at the conversation going on around him during one performance of the Beethoven Quartet, Opus 59), often about subjects that had nothing to do with the recital or concert or opera they had come to hear. Granted that whispering in the Chinese language was an incongruity, the noise level of an audience could reach surprising decibel levels as it was beginning to do in the ballroom now.

A half dozen Chinese teachers from the English department sat at one table with some foreign experts, drinking beer and *qishui*, holding their own private conversation. Other tables added to the babble of tongues, which quieted only slightly as a young Chinese teacher rose and read two poems by Robert Frost. Nevertheless, at the end of his reading, the clapping was generous. Then the Chairman rose and tapped a spoon loudly against his glass to call for order. After a few blessedly brief general observations on the program, he concluded, "I want to thank everyone involved for the Chinese-International cooperation that has made this festival a grand success." After a few additional but brief comments on the fine performances of the participants, Stanley noted gratefully that the Chairman declared the meeting officially closed.

Immediately, some of the *fuwuyuan* could be seen wheeling in from the kitchen a convoy of the heavy stainless steel carts into which they now began piling dirty glasses, empty beer and soda bottles, dirty dishes and table trash. But many of the guests had no intention of leaving so early in the evening. After a few frustrated efforts, the kitchen staff gave up trying to buss the tables, and disappeared back into the kitchen, or just stood around watching the fun, leaving the wide metal carts in the aisles for people to make their way around as best as they could. The drinking and merrymaking went on. An accordion player who appeared was quickly surrounded by a loud, jolly crowd calling out favorite student songs which, red-faced from alcohol, they bellowed out without inhibition. A card game had begun at one of the tables.

Wu Fang's table, led by her now slightly shrill voice, increased the merriment.

"Here! Taste of the nectar. Drink to me with more than just your eyes! I dare you!" Surrounded by admirers, she was in fine fettle. She had removed one of her high heel pumps and poured beer into it, passing it around among the laughing male foreign students around the table. A few Chinese joined in from another table. Holding out their arms, reaching for the shoe, which someone had refilled with beer that now spilled over the side, splashing shirts and hair of the excited male students. Again the shoe was refilled, passed from hand to hand as eager mouths gulped at the foam.

"GANBEI! - BOTTOMS UP!" trumpeted one young man as he grasped the shoe by its heel and tipped it to empty its contents down his throat.

Michel, the French teacher, beyond shyness after many drinks, shouted for someone to pass the shoe to him. Somewhat unsteadily he filled it from the full litre bottle he had been drinking from, and held it high. Shouting "*Heguangle! GANBEI!*" He turned up the shoe to let the liquid pour into his mouth, then tossed it high in the air.

"My heart leaps out to the man I love!" Wu Fang was being her most irresponsible. She was quite tipsy by now. Using one hand to steady herself against a chair back, she mounted it, and quickly leaped onto the table, sending a bottle rolling over the side to crash to the floor. Ignoring the small contretemps, she bowed deeply to Michel, swaying and made more unsteady by having to stand on the table on one high-heeled shoe and one bare foot. She teetered, but undeterred, she twirled, her gold and black silk *qipao* dress twisting about her hips so that the slits, cut to mid-thigh, slanted across her body like a gypsy dancer's gown.

In her element now, she demonstrated a few bumps and grinds for her appreciative audience, then began to belt out a song, transforming herself into an Asian Bette Midler. After only a few bars, she stopped abruptly, as though a thought had occurred to her.

She looked over the room to where Taylor drooped in his chair. Closing her eyes, she raised her arms overhead, and slowly, sensuously, began rotating her body in the exotic Indian dance Stanley had watched her perform in this same ballroom the night of the Autumn Festival. The woman was a fool. She began to sing again, this time in an affectedly high, whiny voice.

"But one man loved the pilgrim soul in me—" Her voice had grown soft and high, as though she had forgotten her audience. She continued to gyrate, oblivious of the din around her. People were laughing and clapping to the rhythm of her voice. The crowd moved back from the table where she danced, to give her stage room. A student tripped against a metal cart nearby, sending it twisting against one of the tables as it spun a wheel. He stopped its motion with a hand, then cursed as he examined himself for injury from the sharp corner he had grabbed.

"—and loved that sorrow in my changing face." Stanley listened with distaste to Wu Fang's parody of Yeats' love poem to Maude Gonne. The woman was outrageous. Now she bent to remove her other slipper. Grasping it by its heel, she shifted into a new mode. Suddenly yelling "Beer! Beer!" she began a dervish dance on the top of the table, waving the slipper about her head. The unsteady boards creaked.

A student obliged her by handing up to her an open bottle of beer. She splashed the amber liquid into the shoe, which she held out toward Taylor.

"Here, Taylor, Taylor baby! Cinderella has something for you!"

She leaned forward, holding the slipper in both hands like a chalice.

Taylor rose from his chair. His lips moved. "You DISGUST me!" His mouth formed the words as he started for the door.

With all her strength, Wu Fang hurled the shoe she was holding toward him, sending beer splashing through the air. As she did so, the top of the big, round mobile table slipped its notch and began to slide on its legs. Wu Fang teetered for an instant. Too late, a student sprang to catch her. With a shriek, she lost balance completely and crashed toward the floor. Blood spurted from her right temple, gushing onto the gold of her dress and mixing with the beer on the floor. She lay motionless.

Falling, she had hit her head, just at the temple, upon the sharp edge of the metal cart. Her black hair fanned over the floor, the section around her temple quickly becoming matted with blood and beer.

She lay still, looking up. But the glazed, staring eyes saw nothing in the living world. The blood continued to flow from the gash at her temple, trickling down the broad cheekbone like party festoons that still moved in the breeze although the dance was over.

Taylor had run forward as he saw Wu Fang fall. He now knelt by her side, white-faced and bewildered. As he raised his head and looked up at the crowd surrounding the scene, as though he sought reassurance that this nightmare was somebody's idea of a joke, a wide insane grin spread over his face, and he began to cry. He felt with both hands in his pockets and found a handkerchief, which he held awkwardly against his wife's temple to stave the blood. He shook her. He called, "Woofy, Woofy" over and over, like a little boy trying to revive a pet dog. Lao Zhao, the Waiban's Deputy Director, appeared from nowhere, followed by several *fuwuyuan*. He placed his hands gently on Taylor's shoulders to draw him away from where Wu Fang lay sprawled on the floor, then bent quickly to read the woman's pulse with two fingers at a wrist. A doctor in the white uniform and barrel-like cap that medical officers wore appeared at the scene. She knelt beside the victim, opening her black bag to remove her stethoscope. Lao Zhao moved to clear the room, gesturing widely with his hands and arms, and in a loud voice admonishing the crowd to leave.

Taylor had been made to sit in a chair. He was shivering very badly, his breath coming in gasps through a sick moaning, when the police arrived.

Chapter 29
A Deed of Dreadful Note

The meeting, called by the Waiban, asked that all foreign teachers attend. Promptly at two o'clock in the afternoon, the Waiban sat ranged like a tribunal in the Conference Room. Yang Youli, impassive as always, was girdled by his deputy and the chief English language translator. Several other Chinese, among them the Party Secretary, talked quietly among themselves. Two police officers were with them, one of them the Chief Inspector of Police, Ling Feng. Standing tall and thin in his white dress uniform with red and gold epaulets, the man contrasted sharply with the drab khaki of his henchman. It was clear that the Chief Inspector's wife (or whoever supervised his wardrobe) had a fond respect for the use of the iron. His shirt and trousers were meticulously pressed. His shoes were polished to a high shine.

Shelby and Elaine entered together, Elaine looking particularly frightened as they passed the two uniformed police attending the door. She hesitated for a moment in the doorway, then, at an abrupt gesture from one of the police, bolted inside and followed after Shelby like a startled lamb. She had been quiet and tense ever since she had explained finally to Shelby the other night that the Waiban had called her into the Foreign Office to investigate quite thoroughly her relationship and dealings with Li Jian. She had been a fool. Now she worried about her own future here, as well as about what would happen to Li Jian.

Taylor was already in the room, sitting alone, looking defeated and forlorn, an abandoned rag doll. It was the first time Shelby had seen him since Woofy's death. He had refused to see anyone from the University, remaining in his closed room excepting when he had been, like the others, escorted downtown for questioning by the police. He was very thin and pale. Chairman Zhang sat close beside him.

Stanley moved from where he had been standing in the doorway and took a seat beside Shelby. She tapped his knee. "What is going on? I'm scared!"

Waiban Director Yang Youli rose from his chair, cleared his throat, and began to speak in Chinese. His voice was loud. Nevertheless, the interpreter sat on the edge of her seat, neck craned toward him as though her life depended on her not missing a word. She translated in a sharp, nervous voice.

"I am very, extremely, sad at what brings us together this afternoon." She paused, then continued, as the Director completed a thought.

"We have been friends working together for a long time for our joint welfare. We have never wished that any evil happening." The interpreter hesitated, evidently searching for the precise, diplomatic, inoffensive words. "We have always wished that our relationship of East and West be of the best. The recent tragic happening, unfortunately in the depths of our life, tragic events will occur." Shelby quivered at the massacre of language. Even in tragedy, yes, bureaucracy reared its head, in this case, its tongue. The Director droned on. Shelby found herself lost in her own thoughts. What a strange year it was turning out to be! When she left her job at Malvern College to come to China for a year's experience, she never thought it would be this kind of experience.

At long last, Yang Youli came to a full, if mechanical, stop. Chief Inspector Ling rose, spoke a few sentences in Chinese, then turned to Stanley, saying in English,

"Professor Poussaint, please explain to your countrymen what we know, and what we have discussed last night."

Poussaint shifted in his chair, and took a moment to look over the notes he had made carefully at the previous night's case meeting to which he had been invited by the Foreign Office and the local police, as the designated representative of the University's English-speaking community. His years in China had polished well his Yale-learned Mandarin which mandated him the spokesman for the small, anxious group that now looked toward him. When he rose, he spoke carefully, choosing his words.

"Everyone regrets the accidental death of Wu Fang, Taylor's wife, this past Saturday. There is great sympathy for Taylor." Heads turned to regard the hunched figure beside Dr. Zhang.

Shelby nudged Elaine, directing her eyes toward Taylor. Although his body drooped in his chair, his gaze was fixed steadfast on Stanley, as though he were trying through some sort of osmotic shock to understand the events that had taken over his life.

"Stanley says he didn't even have to come here this morning, Elaine," she whispered. "He wanted to."

Stanley was continuing, "It has fallen to me to explain to you what the police have uncovered." He nodded deferentially toward Chief Inspector Ling Feng, then looked over his audience. The four Russian experts sat intense, hands clenched at their chests as they focused on the speaker. The Japanese sat straight and impassive in a row in front of the Americans. At last night's meeting with Inspector Ling Feng and the staff of the police force involved in the murder investigation, Stanley had questioned the need or even the advisability of the entire foreign teaching staff of Shi Da being present at this meeting. He had been overruled, told emphatically that it was "Chinese custom to make the facts of all known criminal behavior clear to all those concerned."

Having hesitated for a few seconds as he considered phrasing, Stanley said, "The police have determined that the young teacher Wu Fang was the murderer of Professor Treadway."

He paused. There were a few gasps from his audience.

"Last Sunday morning, apparently Wu Fang and her husband had a tremendous argument during the time they were in the city." He regarded his notes.

"The *fuwuyuan* in the coffee shop where the couple had gone for breakfast were aware of 'red faces and angry voices.' One of the waitresses, who understands a little English, told police the two of them constantly shouted about a 'she.' "'The American man said he will die if he does not know where she has gone'", according to the testimony. At some point, the screaming young Chinese woman, as they referred to Wu Fang, ran out of the restaurant. She was gone for over an hour, while her husband continued to sit in his chair, his head on his arms on the table. Perhaps he fell asleep. No one paid any more attention to him, as lone customers would never be disturbed unless the restaurant was crowded and they really needed the table for waiting customers. The workers went about their business of preparing for the lunch customers. Wu Fang had ample time to accomplish her purpose."

Stanley took a deep breath, moistened his lips, which had gone bone dry during this unpleasant recounting, and looked around the room at the sober, silent group.

"It is—" he hesitated over the choice of a word. "It is inferred from all evidence that, in a fit of rage, she hailed a taxi and returned to the campus. She was seen on campus during this time. She went to Judith's office, argued with her, presumably threatened her and attacked her with a shard of a broken bottle. Unfortunately there are always pieces of broken bottle lying about the campus. In her fit of rage, she just saw and picked up a piece along the way. The Chinese are old hands at using pieces of glass for many purposes." The audience was motionless. Stanley looked over his notes with careful concentration, and spoke slowly, choosing his words with precision.

"The police have asked me to say that they think Wu Fang's intent was not clear: whether she meant to kill Professor Treadway; or, more likely just to wound her for fancied slights and what she thought of as interference in ruining Wu Fang's life with Taylor.

"At any rate, it is clear she stabbed at her like a street urchin with the shard of glass, then ran out, still in a state of paranoid frenzy, slamming the door behind her." Witnesses have testified they heard the door slam and saw her run down the hall and out of the building.

He paused. "Unfortunately her attack severed her victim's carotid artery. Judith Treadway may have tried to call out for help, but the offices are seldom occupied that early on a Sunday morning. Judith probably fainted long before she bled to death. Not that one finds consolation in that. Then, Woofy returned to the restaurant where she had left Taylor, hailing a taxi at the Little Gate. This has been verified by both the bicycle repairman who works constantly at that location and the taxi driver."

The small group still sat tense and sober, listening carefully. Elaine spoke out,

"If Taylor had not been in such an emotional torpor, he would have realized."

"He would not necessarily have realized anything different about his wife's return and subsequent behavior in the restaurant," put in Chief Inspector Ling, speaking in surprisingly good English as he came to Taylor's defense. He had sat down as Stanley made an effort to continue in a moderate voice.

"It's interesting how we all make certain assumptions based on our own expectations." Stanley pushed the reading glasses on his nose to better see his notes. This was not the first quarrel Taylor and Woofy, as you call her, had had in the course of their knowing each other." The Chief Inspector was nodding and stroking his chin as Stanley continued to outline the murder scenario. "Was that not clearly established by the interval in which Taylor sat alone in the restaurant, as he customarily did, waiting for his wife to return?" Ling Feng turned deferentially to Stanley, whom he obviously regarded both as spokesman for the foreigners and as a fellow detective. He raised a hand to signal the speaker.

"Dr. Poussaint, will you please explain in English Woofy's—eh, the woman Wu Fang's—behavior during domestic al-ter-cations?" Although he remained extremely serious, his facial expression displayed his satisfaction at his own command of English.

Stanley continued, as requested, to spell out and clarify the causes of the murder.

"According to Taylor's testimony," he nodded toward that young man, who sat slumped in his seat, his head on his chest, "it was Woofy's habit, in the course of their not-infrequent fights, to take off somewhere, abruptly leaving him to go cry her eyes out or stamp her feet, or, just run around the block a few times, highly charged as she was, for periods of a few minutes to several hours. Then, when played out, she would return to Taylor, whose role seemed to be just to wait patiently for her, wherever they happened to be when she began one of her tirades, whether at a friend's home or in town. Woofy would come back contrite, calm and loving, ready to begin life all over again, as though neither friction nor hostility had occurred between them."

Taylor shifted position in his chair, folding his arms across his chest and stretching his long legs out under the seat in front of him. His mouth gaped open,seemingly in concentration, his attention continued rooted on Stanley.

"On the Sunday of Professor Treadway's murder, her behavior was no different from that on many similar occasions. Possibly," (he emphasized his concession on using that word) "possibly Taylor was so concerned about his own emotional and domestic problems that he seemed to see no relationship between his life and what was happening around him on campus. He's a self-centered lad. I don't think he was even aware that Woofy detested Judith, let alone that she blamed the older woman unreasonably on at least one occasion for becoming involved inadvertently in their personal lives." Stanley did not find it necessary to be specific about the incident of the misguided correspondence from Xiao Mei that Judith had mentioned to him.

"In Wu Fang's distorted view, Judith became the scapegoat, a villain who had interfered in Taylor's and her marriage, and was helping to destroy it.

"Her irrational dislike and resentment of the senior woman, combined with the fear and panic that Taylor would leave her for someone else, was enough to put her over the edge. Her physical hysteria supplied an impetus to rush her back to campus that Sunday morning. I don't know how she knew Professor Treadway was in her office; probably just a guess. It was her habit to work there almost daily, including weekends. Judith preferred that, as it allowed more free time open to students who might wish to see her. That generosity may have cost her her life." He paused, reflecting.

"It took the murderer little time to accomplish an unexpected deed of hysteria and petty malice. Her victim was also a symbol for Wu Fang, a sick woman, of the resentments she bore from her childhood against any world she considered superior to herself. She carried a tremendous chip on her shoulder against

Caucasians, to whom she considered herself inferior."
Stanley concluded, "A classic, tragic case of paranoia."

When Stanley had finished, everyone turned to look at Taylor, who now slumped over in his chair, hands between his knees, a look of pain on his boyish face. At least he's not crying, Stanley mused, recognizing his own unkindness at the thought. The tragic events of the past few days had not—whatever other feelings and strengths they had brought out in Stanley—modified his acute dislike for Taylor, whom he continued to regard as a spoiled brat of a rich kid who always got what he wanted in the end. He was reminded of what Scott Fitzgerald had observed about the rich going through life doing whatever they pleased, and "leaving others to pick up the pieces." He, Stanley, was picking up pieces right now. He was, however, trying conscientiously to be fair to the boy, despite his personal dislike.

Taylor had leaned back in his chair, the fingers of his long bony hands white as they spread out and grasped at his knees. His Adam's apple bobbed nervously. Stanley felt himself wishing he could be sorry for the man. After all, he had just lost a wife. Not that she had been much of an asset; but love can lay claim to the strangest of mandates or, bed partners, as the case may be!

"I tried to tell Woofy, Wu Fang—" Taylor suddenly spoke up. He seemed confused as to how to refer to his dead wife, "—months ago, that our marriage was finished! I couldn't stand her rudeness and surliness. Although she could be quite wonderful at times—" He stopped talking and stared into the distance as though he were reminiscing over the pleasant aspects of his marriage. "But then she would become so rude and cutting!" He raised his arms over his head as though trying to protect himself from physical harm. "I couldn't continue to listen to her constant condemnation of our friends. She disgusted me! But I didn't have the courage to say anything. I was afraid." He flung out his hands palms up, in a pitiful gesture and opened his mouth wide as though he were about to yell. "Ai-ee!" but his voice broke and he squeaked, "I was afraid if I spoke my feelings, she'd do something outrageous!"

"Well, you were certainly right there," said Elaine, who, during the disclosure and explanation of the events surrounding the murder had recovered remarkably well enough from her earlier fears to jump back into the saddle as far as expressing her personal opinions.

With a barely audible "Excuse me, please," Taylor stood abruptly and walked out of the room, his head bowed. He did look as though he were going to cry. The Chief Inspector nodded his head to the sergeant in a motion that directed him to look after the retreating figure. The sergeant saluted and hurried after Taylor. Chairman Zhang immediately rose and followed.

The room was completely still for a moment. Then the Waiban staff, the interpreter and the deputy all rose simultaneously, like an animated video game team responding to a remote control monitor, and filed from the room. The other foreigners rose and were leaving the room in babylons of private discussion. Only Director Yang Youli remained seated, smiling his political smile. With a shake of the head toward Chief Inspector Ling Feng, Shelby exclaimed,

"Oh, I do feel sorry for Taylor. He's such a sweet guy." She leaned back in her chair and crossed her legs prettily. "But I'm still confused."

The teachers still in the room turned to look at her.

"I thought," she blurted, "we were going to be told that a student was the culprit, that's what I thought. That young man, Li Jian." When Shelby had returned to Elaine's flat at her request late Tuesday night, Elaine, hysterical, had finally unburdened herself of her fears. The student Li Jian, with whom she had become more intimate than she should have, she admitted to Shelby, was becoming very threatening and ugly since he could not find his term paper, the plagiarism in which he feared would cause him to be linked to Professor Treadway's murder.

Already last weekend, on the day prior to the murder, he had broken into her office, forcing the door open with the handle of a spoon he had stolen from the student canteen, which he wedged between the door and the cheap lock. He hadn't found the paper in Professor Treadway's office, so he'd cajoled Elaine to talk with her on pretense of being curious to see what the paper looked like, which Elaine had agreed she would do. She would then "lose" the culprit paper.

However, when Judith was murdered the following day, and Li Jian appeared angry and threatening that he still did not have his incriminating paper, Elaine had begun to suspect that he had murdered Judith; and that she would become involved as an accessory, since she knew his motive and had listened to his damning harangues and threats against his foreign teacher.

The Chief Inspector permitted himself to smile. "The student Li Jian was thoroughly investigated, you may be sure. We were well aware of his motives, as well as his actions." He nodded at Stanley, who continued,

"Li Jian may have had murder in his heart. He had himself in a knot of lies that got him into quite enough trouble. Without mayhem, however. As you know, he was desperate to win one of the scholarships to the U.S. Apparently, early on, he got into trouble with Professor Treadway for neglecting to use any sources on his senior thesis. He tried without success to correct his failing before the deadline for the presentation of this important academic paper. When the librarian, Heavenly Fountain, whom we all know, would not permit him to take books out of the library, he began to copy out flat whatever he could get his hands on that seemed to be relevant. But he could not find enough material to satisfy his needs. He then contrived to 'borrow' a paper that, by coincidence, had been written by Wang Jun, a student of mine several years ago, who is now studying in Germany. Apparently my student's little brother made a nice profit selling 'study materials' his big sister left for him at the university."

Shelby sighed. "Li Jian was always very sweet to us, though, wasn't he, Elaine?" Sarcastic and catty though her observation just then was, she felt she was owed that little retribution for the worry and upset Elaine had caused her several days ago in what had turned out to be histrionics over her affair with Li Jian. Thank the Lord it was all over with! What a mystery of manners!

Elaine was curiously quiet for a change. At Shelby's remark, she blushed right down to her collar bone.

There were only five persons still in attendance in the room now, presumably to honor the protocol of escorting Chief Inspector Ling Feng of the Central Prefecture from the University campus, as was polite custom, whenever the police officer was ready to depart. Stanley left it to the Chief Inspector to speak.

"We respect and honor our foreign friends, and their cooperation. With our 'open policy,' there are bound to be some misunderstandings about permissible relations between Chinese and foreigners, of course."

Elaine broke in sourly, "Li Jian. Yeah. I always suspected."

The Chief Inspector cut her. "Yes, Miss Tryst. We know very well of your relations with Li Jian, and how the two of you have been conducting yourselves. He also telephoned you on several occasions saying he must see you about an urgent matter. Then he was detected with you more than once at one o'clock in the morning. We have apprehended him several nights ago as he tried to leave the building. He confessed everything, as well as acknowledging that Miss Tryst had agreed to help him get his false paper back, among other things."

"I—" Elaine reddened again, unable to retort.

The Chief Inspector waved aside any further discussion of the matter. The expression on his face indicated more sternly than words that it was unfortunately not the province of the police at this moment to criticize the morals of a foreign teacher; otherwise, he should have a considerable amount to say to her.

"Li Jian was just, you would say, a silly young man in many ways. He could not resist foreign temptations. He has been severely criticized." He gave her a hard look, from which she turned her face. Then he stood, ending the meeting.

The handshaking and other formalities of leave-taking took a few minutes. Director Yang Youli escorted the Chief Inspector out to his waiting car, both walking erect with the sense of a task well completed.

Stanley only barely suppressed a smile to the Chief Inspector as he passed. He did not suppress a wink at Shelby, who, like the others, had watched Elaine toss her shawl about her shoulders with the air of an offended duchess as she strode alone from the room.

Chapter 30
Right To The End

The entire day had been punctuated by the slsh-slsh of rain that had replaced the snow. November was like that, with its surprising chills and as though it were in constant rebellion against the onset of winter. In the middle of the evening, Stanley sat on the wide sofa in Shelby's apartment. She had asked innumerable questions about Wu Fang and Taylor.

"Poor Woofy!" Shelby came out of her kitchen carrying a small platter of *zha jirou*, an especially delicious deep-fried chicken Lao Wang, the old missionary-trained cook in the Foreign Guest House kitchen, could be wheedled into making when the mood bestirred him. Shelby had the knack of "bestirring" him, having succeeded on several occasions in getting him to cook up for her privately a batch she would bring up from the kitchen after hours and store in her refrigerator for private treats. Now she carried the platter of chicken in one hand, and in the other a bowl of cheddar cheese crackers. She placed both on the cocktail table in front of Stanley.

"Hope you don't mind the ecumenical snack." Her attractive face brightened into a smile as she realized Stanley had stopped talking and was licking his lips at the sight of the chicken. She seated herself in an armchair opposite, curling her legs up under her in her favorite position.

"Umm-mm." He picked up a wing and waved it in the air in approval before taking a bite, which he chewed with apparent delight, then swallowed. Only after this demonstration of the bon vivant did he go on with what he had been saying.

"Woofy was pretty vindictive. And cunning." He looked around for a place to put down the chicken bone, spied the paper cocktail napkins on the table and provided himself with one on which he not uncarefully wiped his fingers and disposed of the bone, while continuing to talk. "Chairman Zhang says that, unknown to Taylor, Woofy arranged a meeting with Xiao Mei, then intimidated that naïve young woman into going to the countryside to have an abortion, and afterwards stay out of the picture." He munched at a cheese cracker.

"Woofy had frightened Xiao Mei into believing that if she did not leave town, she herself, as a cheated wife, would go to the department chairman, and divulge the whole shameful story of the 'adulterous affair.' Xiao Mei, a simple, romantic young country girl brought up in Chinese tradition, believed that the embarrassment, the loss of face for her beloved Taylor when it was found out that he had seduced one of his students, would be unbearable."

"As well it might be!" Stanley shook his head. "Especially in this country where sexual mores remain largely strict and puritanical, even if there has been considerable loosening up recently! No, Woofy was able very easily to frighten Xiao Mei, who then left campus, not telling anyone where she was going." Stanley recalled the day he had approached her at the end of a class asking about her leaving campus, and she had fled with only a murmured "tonight," her face pale, eyes frightened.

"How did they find out where Xiao Mei had gone if she didn't tell anybody?"

"Fortunately, the Chairman recalled that Xiao Mei's grandparents came from a village in Jilin Province. He knows the area rather well, had once spent a season there assigned to a farm during the Cultural Revolution. Through the local authorities, he was able to locate the old grandmother who had brought up Xiao Mei. Xiao Mei is there in her grandmother's cottage, a fact that would not have gone unobserved for long in a busy-nosed village. She seems to be well."

In response to Shelby's interrogative raise of the eyebrows, he added, "No, I know nothing about an abortion, if there was one." He dipped into the cheese crackers and went on, as though there were more significant elements to attach the mind to than the status of the young woman's pregnancy.

"Wu Fang made one big mistake, however. In her eagerness to clear any traces of Taylor's affair, she made her way into Judith's flat after Judith's death, to look for the envelope of a letter Xiao Mei had sent to Taylor. It was a letter that had caused great trouble because it had been placed by mistake in Judith's pigeon hole, number forty-five in the English department administrative office instead of number forty-six, which is Taylor's slot right beside it." He hesitated, deciding whether to tell Shelby that he had seen Wu Fang come into Judith's room to retrieve the envelope the day he himself had gone there trying to ascertain whether Li Jian's plagiarized paper was still among the others, or whether Professor Treadway had returned the failed paper to the student, thus possibly fanning flames of disappointment and resentment. Stanley decided it was not necessary to make Shelby privy to that information. Let her rest secure in the belief that the police had solved the crime on their own, that he was merely a go-between in language relations between the foreigners and the local police. Which in truth he was. His own bit of detecting, although welcomed by his friend the Inspector, had been unsolicited.

"As it happened," he continued smoothly, "Judith told me about the letter shortly after she received it. The fact that we have so many of the same students often led us to discussions about them, those usually pertaining to their work, I should add, and not their personal lives. Were it the latter, we might have known about Xiao Mei and Taylor earlier."

"At any rate, in Wu Fang's case, it seemed apparent that only a very desperate person would sneak into the dead woman's room to retrieve a piece of evidence that might reveal a motive. That piece of information was all the police needed to make a connection with Xiao Mei. It was she who, when found at her grandmother's cottage, revealed Wu Fang's threats. Although most angry people don't carry out their threat to kill," Stanley added wryly.

Shelby gave him a keen glance. "My, the police have surely been active," she offered. She crossed her legs prettily. "Please go on."

He continued without comment. "The identification and statement of the taxi driver who drove Woofy back to the restaurant from campus, and of the *fuwuyuan* who identified her as the teacher she had seen in the office corridor that fateful Sunday morning, provided strong circumstantial evidence. But Woofy would not confess. The police had repeatedly questioned her, but there was not enough evidence for an arrest.

"Woofy was aware of this and exploited it, boasting to Taylor that she knew who had 'gotten rid of our enemy,' seeming to implicate Xiao Mei as Judith's murderer, though without actually mentioning her. Taylor of course would not nor could not say anything to the police. He was a very stressed young man by this time. He knew his wife's eccentricities and highly emotional behavior long before he began distancing himself from her because of his loss of Xiao Mei. His guilt over his past affair nevertheless kept him in a constant state of ambivalence. He loved and hated his wife. He did not have the moral strength to pry himself loose from her." Stanley paused to take a sip of his drink.

"As you well know, Wu Fang could not tolerate being looked down on by the Anglo-Saxon contingent, the 'blond and blue-eyed,' in Thomas Mann's phrase. Judith, in particular, in the dining hall, had publicly denigrated her "new" teaching methods, and criticized Woofy for her rudeness toward Michel and some of the foreign students, accusing her of bullying them.

"Taylor told Inspector Ling Feng about her highly-charged emotional reaction to Judith's laughing when Woofy had first appeared with her hair cropped in the latest fashion, the result on Wu Fang's part of what was probably an agonized decision to cut off the long traditional braid she had worn since the end of her rebellious adolescent days. You'll recall, Shelby," Stanley said as he picked up another cheese cracker and popped it into his mouth, "Woofy once told us a story about how her mother had cried when she had learned of her teenage daughter's effort to become 'American' and 'modern' at the expense of her own family tradition. Well," he paused, "to be snickered at and be told she looked like a boy was more than she could tolerate—she, who wanted desperately to be accepted, to pass, in her distorted vision, into the forefront of a revolutionary new world."

Shelby moved across to the other end of the sofa on which Stanley sat. She bobbed her head in agreement as he spoke, one hand cupped under her chin, very absorbed in what he was relating.

"But how did the police prove it was really she who did the stabbing? Don't they have to be sure?"

"The case might never have been resolved if a crucial piece of evidence had not been turned up the day of the poetry party. Because of the many outside guests who were invited, the department *fuwuyuans* had been ordered to clean thoroughly the bathrooms and adjoining storage spaces so that everything would look spick and span for the festivities. In a dark corner behind the entrance to the women's toilets, one of them found, buried in a bag of sawdust, an unusually large shard of green bottle glass. The sawdust, incidentally, is used only occasionally as a cleaning agent on the stone floors. Since the *fuwuyuan*, like the rest of the staff, knew that broken glass had been the weapon used to murder Professor Treadway, she immediately took the piece to the police."

She interrupted, "How did you find that out, Stanley?" She gave him a most winsome smile. "Or shouldn't I ask?"

"You may ask." He liked her investigative reporter attitude. "For all the good it will do you!"

"You don't fool me. Your friends the cops tell you things." She raised an eyebrow at him.

He winked at her. "Do you want me to go on, or not?"

"Of course I do!"

"Well," Stanley considered what remained of the facts that he could relate. "In her haste and state of mind that Sunday morning, Wu Fang had not bothered to remove her fingerprints from the glass. The police were about to arrest her at the poetry festival Thursday evening, when she slipped and fell off the table to her death."

Shelby shifted her legs under her on the sofa, and shivered. After a moment, she said,

"If the affair between Taylor and Xiao Mei had been going on since last September, how come it took Woofy so long to find out?"

"You know the old saying, 'Wives are always the last to know.' That certainly held true here. If it hadn't been for the letter, she may not have found out at all for a long time. Maybe not ever, if things had worked out differently. Theirs doesn't sound like a marriage made to last!"

Shelby rose to answer a knock at the door. "Chairman Zhang!"

"I am sorry to disturb you." The Chairman stood in the doorway, as diffident as one of his students. "I shall not bother you long." Wearing padded trousers and an old brown tweed greatcoat that hung below his knees (he must have owned that coat for forty years! Shelby thought,) Dr. Zhang looked a little like an outsize snowman. On his head was a Mongolian fur hat with earflaps, a hat referred to as the "local thermometer": if the flaps were tied up over the crown, the weather was comparatively warm; ear flaps down, but untied under the chin, as his was now, meant somewhat cold weather. Flaps tied at the chin, very cold; fur flap at the forehead also down, bitter cold. Local conventional wisdom held that by looking out a window at fur-hatted passersby at any time of day, one could get an accurate reading of the temperature out of doors at that time.

Stanley said, "It must have stopped raining."

"It's beginning to snow." Dr. Zhang grinned. "I am prepared for all weather, you see!"

At Shelby's insistence he removed the cumbersome coat and hat, sat down, and accepted a cup of tea. After only one refusal. We've made some progress in westernizing the institution! Shelby smiled to her, reminded of the story of the disappointed young Chinese student in America who had the opportunity to refuse just one time a slice of desired chocolate cake before it was removed from the table.

"I apologize for visiting you unannounced," Chairman Zhang said. "It is very discourteous. But these are unusual times. I hope you will forgive me."

Shelby waved a small hand. "*Meiguanxi*, no problem. *Women shi pengyou*, we are friends."

It was the first time Stanley had heard Shelby speak any Chinese. He liked her accent.

The Chairman said, "The *fuwuyuan* at the desk downstairs told me I would find you here in Miss Johnson's room, Stanley. I came to the Guest House earlier this evening to deliver a telegram to Taylor. It is from Xiao Mei."

At the news of a telegram, Shelby glanced at Stanley with raised eyebrows. He seemed not at all surprised at what to her was startling news.

"She is on her way here. Taylor has now gone to meet her at the train." The Chairman sipped his tea. The merest smile appeared on his smooth face, but was instantly gone.

"They will not stay here, of course. That would not be acceptable behavior. We must consider the students."

"Dr. Zhang," asked Shelby, "when did you first find out about Xiao Mei and Taylor? No one seemed to know anything about their relationship until very recently."

The Chairman nodded sagely.

"Actually, probably half the department knew about it, I suspect." He allowed himself a smile. "For months, I have watched Taylor and Xiao Mei in the corridors, in the way of lovers hiding behind columns and doors to gaze soulfully at each other when they thought no one was nearby. The Political Unit finally criticized Xiao Mei for this. She was about to be asked to leave the University, and to be sent to another city. Such behavior as hers is not usually condoned."

"But none of us had any idea!" Shelby emphasized the "us."

"The Chinese are good about keeping secrets from foreigners. However," he added, wiping his forehead with a clean white handkerchief that he took from his pocket, "this was not to be the case here."

"But will they be allowed to marry?"

"Yes. They will go to the Registry tomorrow. They seem to have found joy in each other and wish very much to marry. It will not be forbidden. Fortunately it is the twenty-first century and not the 1970's. It is not a major problem these days for a Chinese to marry a foreigner. Her grandmother in the countryside will probably have the traditional objections, but, considering the circumstances, they are lucky. Everything has been arranged."

Carefully, he folded and replaced the handkerchief in his inner coat pocket as he rose, retrieved his coat and hat from a chair where Shelby had laid them, and prepared to leave.

"You will not see them again soon, but they will be happy. Taylor asked me to tell you good-bye."

When Chairman Zhang had left, Shelby said,

"Well, I think I need some Mango Tang. What about you, Stanley?" As she started for the kitchen, she turned and added, "I think you've been in on a lot more information around here than you let on." She dimpled.

Men, by their nature, enjoy talking about themselves, especially to a willing and pretty listener. Stanley was no exception. To the offer of Mango Tang, he nodded assent agreeably. He stood up, stretched, and walked across the room to pull aside the textured forest-green linen drapes at Shelby's window. Excellent taste in drapes! He stood silently observing snowflakes break against the window pane, melt and disappear. As he watched, the snow metamorphosed into the slow rain of earlier in the day. He closed the drapes.

Every decade, he mused, thinking over what Dr. Zhang had said about the twenty- first century being a more liberal time for the country, the Chinese renounce thirty years of the past and reinvent themselves, becoming more what they are with each transformation. This leads to intricate and fascinating mystery.

He looked toward the kitchen to see where Shelby had disappeared. He'd like to share this idea with her. He loved China. Goddamnit, he loved it! It was like no other country he knew. He returned to the sofa and leaned back comfortably, listening to the rainfall. He helped himself to a crisp chicken leg and waited for Shelby to come back into the sitting room. He complimented himself for having already prepared for his eight o'clock class in the morning.

ISBN 141201180-9

9 781412 011808